"You can call me anytime. Night or day."

Desi lifted her head. Her sideways gaze, her blue eyes shadowed by luxurious lashes, turned him to mush. If she suggested chaining him at her front door like a watchdog, he'd do it.

"Are you hitting on me?" Her voice held a smoky note.

"Do you want me to?"

She dropped her gaze. "No."

No surprise, but it was disappointing. Bench-pressing a hundred and fifty pounds took less effort than it took to pull his hand away. "Too bad. The offer stands anyway. Call me night or day. I live to protect and serve."

SHERYL LYNN

MIDNIGHT INVESTIGATION

HARLEQUIN®

TORONTO • NEW YORK • LONDON
AMSTERDAM • PARIS • SYDNEY • HAMBURG
STOCKHOLM • ATHENS • TOKYO • MILAN • MADRID
PRAGUE • WARSAW • BUDAPEST • AUCKLAND

A very special thank you to Becky Agronow, Marina Bridges, Diane Gratzmiller, Sandi Kraley and Colleen Palmer, who poked and prodded me to write this book. You goils are the best. My eternal gratitude goes to Marylin Warner, the best writing buddy ever, who undangles my modifiers and keeps me laughing.

Thank you, too, to my wonderful Tom and Abby, who only gripe a little bit about me writing instead of cooking. And thank you, Tristan, for bringing the lovely Heidi into the fold.

A special shout-out goes to the gang at steve-o-meter.com for all their support and goofiness. Props to you all. Last, but not least, thank you Jason Hawes and Grant Wilson of the Atlantic Paranormal Society. You guys don't know me, but you sure inspire me.

Recycling programs for this product may not exist in your area.

ISBN-13: 978-0-373-88913-6

MIDNIGHT INVESTIGATION

Copyright © 2009 by Jaye W. Manus

www.eHarlequin.com

Printed in U.S.A.

ABOUT THE AUTHOR

Sheryl Lynn lives in Colorado with her husband of almost thirty years, two oversized dogs and three crazy cats. When not writing Intrigue novels, she's writing articles for steve-o-meter.com or making bead art and jewelry. If you want to say hi, contact her at sheryl.lynn_intrigue@yahoo.com.

Books by Sheryl Lynn

CAST OF CHARACTERS

Desi Hollyhock—A paranormal investigator with a skeptical eye and a knack for debunking ghosts.

Buck Walker—A cop with a secret—he can talk to the dead.

Gwen Hollyhock—Desi's sister wants nothing more than to see a ghost.

Dallas Stone—Founder of the Rocky Mountain Paranormal Research Team, he's on a quest to find the truth.

Mary Hollyhock—She loves her granddaughters and wants to help them in times of need.

Charles and Veronica Skillihorn—Their tragedy continues even after death.

The Dark Presence—A murderous ghost whose jealousy makes him deadly.

Chapter One

"I'm not a forgiving person." Desi Hollyhock focused her sternest look on the newest member of the Rocky Mountain Paranormal Research Team, or Rampart, as they were known. "Rampart is all about scientific method. None of that woo-woo stuff. One strike and you're out. Got it?"

Buck Walker nodded.

Desi kept her voice barely above a whisper, but she figured the recorders had picked up her words anyway. Big deal. Everyone knew she did not want a psychic on the team. Just because she'd been outvoted did not mean she had to put up with nonsense.

So far Buck had behaved himself. He'd helped the team set up cameras and recorders in this supposedly haunted house near downtown Colorado Springs. Quietly attentive, he listened to explanations about why recorders were placed in certain locations. His job was to learn, and he took it seriously. Neither the house's creepy atmosphere nor working in darkness fazed him.

He focused now on a handheld digital video recorder. It was a night-vision camera that magnified even the faintest light source. The glow from the viewing screen illuminated his face. He had a penlight hooked beneath his pinkie finger, and its thin beam pointed at her shoes.

"Safety first," she said. "Watch where you put your feet. Watch your head. Stick with me. We work in pairs so we can corroborate personal experiences. We keep each other calm, too. If you get freaked out, let me know."

"I won't get freaked out," he said.

"Everybody gets spooked. Eventually." She pointed her flashlight in the direction of the infrared camera taped atop a stepladder. "Stay away from the power cords. Keep your voice down, especially when you're near a digital recorder. They are very sensitive."

"Yes, ma'am," he said. The corners of his mouth twitched.

Did he laugh at her? It was bad enough that his height emphasized her lack of it, and bad enough the other female members of the team had indulged in raunchy comments about his dark good looks and buff body, but mostly she resented getting stuck training a guy who claimed psychic ability.

"I am a police officer," he said. "I'm used to working in the dark." He smiled, his calm, controlled air saying, *Do your best. You can't rattle me.* "Why are we working in the dark, anyway? Spirits are just as active in daylight."

Spirits, she thought with disgust. "It's practical. There are fewer people around, less electrical use and outside noise to interfere with the equipment. Not so many nosy neighbors trying to see what we're up to. Most of our clients do not want others to know they're having paranormal experiences. It's a pain sometimes." She held up a small digital camera. "I'll warn you when I'm going to take a picture. I'll say 'flash.' Close your eyes so you aren't blinded. Any questions?"

"What's the best way to use this camera?"

"Hold it close, right under your breastbone."

He raised the camera a few inches.

"Let it move with your body so it sees what you see. Keep your movements smooth and stay aware. You don't want to forget you're holding it and end up with a movie starring the floor."

He turned slowly, taking in the big room, his gaze intent on the black-and-white image on the viewing screen.

She turned slowly, too, examining the room that took up the entire third floor. Six Rampart members were investigating tonight. Tony and Tara were outside in the step-side van that served as the command center, watching the IR camera monitors and making sure the equipment didn't glitch. Desi and Buck investigated the second and third floors, while Dallas and Ringo took the first floor and basement. In about two hours the teams would rotate.

This house had a sad history. Built in the 1880s,

it had been a monument to a silver miner's hard work and perseverance in the harsh Rocky Mountains. Since the 1950s it had sat empty—except for brief occupancies by tenants—slowly strangled by overgrown ivy and worn by the elements. The city had been on the verge of condemning it and having it torn down when the current owners, the Moores, bought it with high hopes of restoring it to its former glory.

The Moores had begged the Rocky Mountain Paranormal Research Team for help. They insisted the house was haunted. The activity was so frightening the Moores were ready to walk away and to hell with the money and work they'd invested.

Desi shone her flashlight at debris piled under a window. The walls were in various stages of undress, with patches of hideous cabbage-rose wallpaper, areas of missing plaster with lathing bared like bones, and large sections where the framing showed. The wooden floor was painted. Where interior walls had been removed, the beautiful original oak flooring was revealed. The Moores' bed sat in a clean, uncluttered corner near a fancy little fireplace with Van Briggle tiles and a cast-iron screen.

"What are we looking for?" Buck asked.

"The Moores have owned the place a year, but only moved in about a month ago. They had to put on a new roof, completely redo the plumbing and install a furnace before the place was livable. Activity started as soon as they moved in. They hear voices and other noises, and somebody moving around."

Desi pointed the light at the corner near the bathroom door. "They've seen a figure that moves from there and across the windows, blocking the light."

She worked her cold toes inside her sneakers. The room stank of chemicals and that sour funk old houses acquired after decades of absorbing odors. She examined an exposed framing timber. Black streaks and splotches marked water damage.

"Mrs. Moore claims something chokes her while she sleeps." She then warned him: "Flash." She took several pictures of the moldy walls. She photographed the high ceiling where telltale water stains spread from the coving.

Her walkie-talkie crackled. "Desi? This is Dallas."

She unhooked it from her belt and thumbed the Transmit button. She spoke closely into the unit, keeping her voice down. "I'm here. Go ahead."

"Are you still up on the third floor?"

"Sure are. The walls are full of mold. With all the chemicals and dust it's no wonder the Moores say the place feels oppressive. It even feels creepy to me. It could account for her nightmares and sensation of being choked."

"The basement is pretty bad, too," Dallas said. "The electrical is a mess. Wires everywhere. The EMF readings are through the roof."

Focused on the camera screen, Buck made his way slowly around the cavernous room. The camera light gave him a corona, outlining his body. He had exceptionally broad shoulders. His waist and hips were lean, and his legs were long. Calvin Klein would loved to have this guy model in one of those sexed-up jeans ads.

"You haven't left the third floor? Been on the stairs?"

Dallas's voice through the walkie-talkie startled her. She scowled at where her mind had wandered. "Not at all. Third floor only."

"We heard someone walking around in the kitchen. We're going to check it out."

She hooked the unit back on her belt. A shiver ran through her. Even with a thermal shirt and a heavy sweatshirt, she had goose bumps. The walls and windows leaked icy air.

Buck asked, "What does the EMF meter do again?"

"It detects electromagnetic fields. The theory is that spirits need energy to manifest. If there are spikes in the readings, it could be because something is about to happen. A lot of people are sensitive to high EMFs. It can cause nausea, dizziness, flu-like symptoms, depression, even hallucinations."

She resumed documenting mold, places where heavy-duty paint strippers had been used on the woodwork and power outlets. She slipped the camera into a pocket and from another pulled out an EMF meter. She slowly swept the room. Even around the power outlets the meter barely moved.

Buck asked, "Have you ever seen a ghost?"

The question irritated her, but his voice took the

edge off. Low and even with rich tones and careful enunciation, his was a voice to make a person sit up and pay attention. She needed to be firm, let him know she was in charge and that this wasn't a Halloween spook game they played. His smooth voice made her sound like a harpy by comparison. She wanted him to take her seriously, not think she was a bitch.

She forced a smile, determined to be professional and friendly. "I've never had any kind of personal experience. Nothing I can't explain, anyway."

"Do you hope to see a ghost?"

"This is research. It's about gathering enough evidence to prove the paranormal is more than superstition and ghost stories. It's also about ferreting out the hoaxes and scam artists."

Especially phony psychics, she thought.

A creaking noise froze Desi in her tracks. Buck froze, too.

She focused her flashlight on the bedroom door. It hadn't moved.

"It sounded like it came from the bathroom," Buck whispered.

Another creak. There was no mistaking the eerie protest of rusty hinges as a door slowly opened.

BUCK HELD THE CAMERA steady on Desi while she examined the bathroom. A sensation akin to spiderwebs being dragged across skin tickled his nerves. This old house was definitely haunted.

He'd found the Rocky Mountain Paranormal

Research Team Web site on the Internet. Their organization impressed him. Like Desi said, no woo-woo stuff. They sought evidence through scientific methods and counted numerous debunked hoaxes among their successes. It had taken Buck months to work up the nerve to contact Dallas Stone, founder and leader of the team.

After hearing Buck's story, Dallas had set up a reading, with himself as the subject. Buck didn't talk to people about his ability, and he only initiated contact with spirits when he sensed a compelling need. He didn't know how to conduct a reading. Buck had been nervous and embarrassed, which worsened as Dallas sat in stony silence, his arms crossed and his body language controlled.

Finally, feeling like a fool, Buck had said, "If there's anybody here who'd like to talk to Dallas, I can hear you." He'd half hoped no spirits would show. Then they could have a good laugh, and Buck could apologize for wasting their time and leave, never to return. A male entity had shown up and shared one of Dallas's secrets. When Buck revealed it, Dallas—a no-nonsense type, macho through and through—had broken down in tears.

Dallas had then surprised Buck by inviting him to join the team.

"They did a nice job in here," Desi whispered. "Can you imagine how much it costs to renovate one of these old houses?"

The first time he'd met Desi Hollyhock, she'd

swaggered into the room like a pirate and talked as tough as any veteran cop. Her attitude was what cops liked to call Taser bait. It might have unnerved him if she weren't so tiny. He bet she had to stretch to claim more than three inches over five feet tall. He put her weight at one-ten, tops. Right now, in a bulky sweatshirt and cargo pants with multiple pockets bulging with ghost-hunting accessories, she looked like a little kid wearing her big brother's clothing.

He kept the camera focused on her as she opened and closed every cabinet and drawer. The hinges and slides were silent.

The camera picked up every reflection so the sheen off her smooth, dark hair made it look blond on the screen. Her eyes had a silvery glow. Those crystal-blue eyes, so striking with her dark hair and pale skin, were burned into his memory. Eyes alive with energy and intelligence. Eyes that made him want to see how deep the toughness went.

Sexy.

Not so sexy was her dislike for psychics and mediums. A dislike so deep and contemptuous it sounded like a phobia. He'd been subjected to skepticism, scoffing, fear and, worst of all, painful hopefulness that his gift—curse—could solve problems. But Desi acted as if his very existence offended her.

He heard voices.

Desi froze, her head cocked. "Did you hear something?"

"Sounded like people talking."

They heard faint laughter.

"I know that laugh. It's Ringo." Desi crouched next to the vanity, where a large floor vent was covered by a fancy-work grill. She held her hand over the vent. "No wonder it's so cold up here. There's barely any hot air coming through." She pulled the walkie-talkie off her belt. "Dallas? Desi here. Where are you?"

Buck leaned in to better see the vent. He caught the scent of Desi's hair, a mixture of sweetness and tang. He backed away.

"Basement. Furnace room. Where are you?"

"Still on the third floor, and we can hear you through the vent. Are there any doors?"

"One wall is covered with cabinets."

"Check the doors, would you?"

In a few seconds came the eerie creak of old hinges.

"That's it!" Desi exclaimed.

"It's loose," Dallas said. "It won't stay closed."

"Did the furnace come on within the last few minutes?"

"As a matter of fact, it did. Ah ha! The sudden rush of air moved the door?"

"That's exactly what I'm thinking. This vent must come straight from the furnace room. It makes it sound like there's a door opening in here." She flashed a big smile at Buck. "Mystery solved."

Her smile struck him right in the heart. It made her beautiful.

"All right," she said. "We're going to do some EVP work."

"Wait," Dallas said. "Do you have a K2 meter?"

Desi said, "I do, but it only works for you and Ringo."

"Exactly," Dallas said. "It's making me paranoid that Ringo is working some kind of hoodoo on it."

Ringo's "Hey!" drifted through the vent.

"I'll give it a shot." Desi rose to her feet. In the main room she headed for the bed. She set the digital recorder on the quilted coverlet. Velcro ripped and she reached into a deep pocket on her pants.

Buck peered at the unit she held. It was about ten inches long in a plastic case and had a bank of glass bulbs.

"Electricians use them," she said. "Dallas gets some interesting results with it. Me?" She shrugged. She turned it on and the glass bulbs lit up one by one, flashing from yellow to green to red. It darkened. She set the unit near the digital recorder.

The paranormal researchers had more gadgets than a patrol car. "What does it do?" Buck asked.

"Measures magnetic fields. Dallas and Ringo keep getting what looks like intelligent responses through it."

An image of a wooden rocking horse flashed through Buck's mind. Eyes half-closed, he listened with his inner ear. The entity felt friendly and very young, and it was aware of Buck and Desi. Another image danced in and out of his consciousness. A striped rubber ball, the paint rubbed away by use.

Buck and Dallas had talked at length about how they might use Buck's ability in investigations. The discussion regarding the Moore house focused solely on Buck needing to learn about the research equipment and how to conduct an investigation. Dallas hadn't told Buck what to do if he saw or felt something in this house. Buck took seriously Desi's warning against woo-woo stuff.

The spirit felt playful and curious. Buck moved closer to the door, attempting to pinpoint the spirit's energy with the camera. He said, barely a whisper, "I know you're here. I see your toys."

Coldness blanketed Buck's skin as the ghost's delight sparked through Buck like static electricity. A pang of pity tightened his chest. Ghosts needed to move on, release or be released from this plane of existence. They had families and loved ones on the Other Side, or so he hoped. Children's ghosts saddened him. They were lost and too far from home.

"Bring the camera over here," Desi said. "Let's do some EVP work."

"If you don't believe in ghosts," he said to Desi, "why do you do this?"

Desi sat on the edge of the bed. "Belief is for church." She lifted her chin. "Either I know or I don't know, and whatever I claim to know better be backed up by hard evidence. I'm looking for facts. Anecdotes and sightings are interesting, but they don't mean squat as proof. You're filming the floor."

He jerked the camera up to level.

She pointed at the nightstand. "Set the camera over there. Focus it on the K2."

Buck was familiar with EVPs—electronic voice phenomena—where recording equipment picked up disembodied voices the human ear could not.

A man said over the walkie-talkie, "Desi? Tony here. Check the IR camera on the third floor. See if a cord got knocked loose. It's acting up."

Buck didn't envy Tony's position in the command center van. Colorado was in the grip of a cold snap. It had been over a week since the temperature had made it above zero. He wasn't looking forward to his turn in the command center.

Desi tested the power and line cords to the IR camera. She spoke into the walkie-talkie. "Everything is fine here. What's it doing?"

"Cutting in and out. Never mind, it's working now. Shees, hope it's not the computer. How's Buck doing? Being a good soldier?" Tony's laugh sounded like a cackle over the unit. "Tell him if he survives a night with you, I'll buy him a beer."

Buck chuckled. He felt the brush of a ghostly hand against his fingers and the youthful spirit seemed to laugh, too.

"Shut up, Tony." Desi hooked the unit on her belt. She returned to the bed and crossed her arms, looking at the digital recorder and K2 meter. "Is there anyone here who'd like to speak with us?"

Buck glimpsed a glow near Desi's face, a ghostly outline of a boyish cheek. Buck's mouth twisted in bemusement. Spirits couldn't read his mind, so he had to speak to communicate. He wanted to ask the ghost why he was here, and why he would not or could not leave.

"I'm Desi and this is Buck. We aren't here to bother you or harm you in any way. If you want to talk to us we have equipment here that can help you."

The ghostly glow hovered over the digital recorder. A wispy hand touched it.

Buck said, "May I ask a question?" He really wanted to ask why she disliked him so much. Most people got to know him, at least a little, before declaring him scum.

She gestured at the digital recorder.

"Do you like being here?" he asked.

A smile flashed, revealing a missing front tooth. Buck sighed unhappily. This child had been very young when he died. Buck's theory was that a parent's grief prevented the spirits of children from passing to the Other Side.

"Do you like what the people who live here are doing to the house?"

He got a clear vision of a playroom with striped curtains, a shelf of books and the wooden rocking horse. He caught himself before asking if the child missed his toys. "Would you like it better if they fixed up a room for you?"

"Buck!" Desi hissed. Instead of glaring at him over his dumb question, she smiled.

"Did you see that?" She focused her flashlight on

the K2 meter. "It lit up." She looked around the room. "Can you make the lights go on again?" One, then two bulbs flickered with weak yellow lights. Desi clamped a hand over her mouth, but part of a giggle escaped.

The spirit glow flared, bursting with delight, showing a broad, gap-toothed smile and shining eyes. The child had found a new toy.

"Get really close to this device," Desi said. "See if you can make it light up again." Desi's flashlight dimmed, then died. The entire bank of bulbs on the K2 lit up. "Did you live in this house? Answer yes with the lights. If it's no, leave it dark." The K2 blazed.

Desi laughed. "Unreal! I have never been able to get it to do that." She snapped a hard look at Buck. "Hey, is Dallas playing a joke on me? Are you helping him set me up?"

"No, ma'am. I swear. That thing is definitely picking up the…something."

"Freaky," she muttered. "Are you a woman who used to live here?"

Nothing.

"Are you the man who built the house?"

Nothing.

Desi pulled a disgusted face. "Figures. An anomaly." She shook her flashlight. It was dead.

Buck asked, "Are you a boy?"

The bank of bulbs lit up.

Buck's penlight died. He shook it and pressed the

button a few times. The only light came from the DVR camera screen and from outside street lamps shining through the windows. Spirits needed energy in order to manifest and interact with the physical world. Batteries were an easy source of energy.

Buck struggled to come up with yes and no questions Desi wouldn't consider woo-woo. They learned the child was nine years old. He had three sisters and two brothers. He was the youngest. He liked this house. He liked the people who lived here.

Desi waved at Buck to be quiet. Buck thought for somebody who scoffed at ghosts, she was certainly excited about talking to one. "Are you the one making noises?" She asked. One bulb barely flickered. "Does that mean you only make a little bit of noise?" A definite yes. "Are there others with you?"

Heaviness settled around Buck like a heavy velvet curtain. A feeling so oppressive, so…angry, it made him dizzy. The little boy's spirit fled. Desi's questions seemed muffled, as if sound waves had to swim through sludge to reach his ears.

Buck turned his head slowly. He spotted it in the corner by the bathroom door. A Dark Presence. His mouth filled with dust and his skin crawled. He kept his head down, not looking directly at the shadow within a shadow.

"Are you lonesome?" Desi asked.

Buck mentally begged her to shut up. If he warned her, it would notice him. It would know he could see and it would focus on him. It moved toward Desi. It flowed, absorbing the thin light as it passed the windows, slithering along the wall, powered by malevolence. They needed to get out of here. He could not let it notice him. Could not allow its dark attention to focus on him. Could not allow it to pick and probe at his mind.

The glow of the handheld camera vanished, plunging the room into darkness.

At the same time, Desi said, "You poor thing. Why don't you come home with me?"

Chapter Two

Buck sensed the Dark Presence's sick interest in Desi's invitation. He stepped between it and Desi, clenched his fists and shouted, "Get out!"

It lacked face and form, but Buck felt its dark attention focus on him. Its dark energy surrounded Buck, pressed on his chest and head as if a giant vise had clamped him in its jaws. His muscles quivered.

"Get out of here! Get out! You don't belong here."

"I thought you weren't scared of the dark," Desi said. Metal clinked against metal as she shook dead batteries out of her flashlight. "Calm down. Take a deep breath."

"I'm not talking to you," he said. "I can't believe you asked that thing to come home with you." He faced it, blocking Desi from its malignant attention.

"Oh, please, it was a joke." Her flashlight brightened. She rose from the bed. "You have to calm down. Do you need to go outside?"

It disappeared. The room felt empty, tomb-like. Buck struggled to control his breathing and racing heart. Relief weakened his entire body, and his joints ached with the sudden drop in adrenaline. Icy fear remained. It had seen him and it knew what he was. Knew he could be used.

A touch on his arm made him flinch. Desi folded her small hand around his forearm. "What in the world is wrong with you?"

Underlit by the flashlight her face was harshly shadowed and openly concerned. But she was not, Buck knew, concerned about the right thing. "Don't you know what you just did? You're supposed to be experienced. You're supposed to know!"

She went rigid, fairly vibrating with anger. "I *am* experienced."

He searched the shadows and listened hard with his inner ear. It felt gone. He prayed it was gone. "That was the stupidest thing you could have done. You have no idea what's in this house!"

Footsteps clomped up the stairs, startling them both. Dallas called, "Desi? You aren't answering the walkie-talkie. Desi? Buck?"

"Power drain," she called in reply. She shot Buck a withering glare and left the room.

AT THE HEADQUARTERS of the Rocky Mountain Paranormal Research Team, in the windowless tech room, Desi rested her forearms on the back of Dallas Stone's chair. Dallas and Ringo, with some help from other members, had spent the last week watching every second of footage from the IR cameras and handhelds, and listening to every audio recording from the eight hours the team had spent investigating the Moores' house.

Desi thought the investigation had been a train wreck. After babbling about dark entities, Buck had left the house and refused to go back inside. A big bad cop, unafraid of the dark. Right. He'd spent the rest of the investigation in the command center van.

When he told Dallas the place had two ghosts, one friendly and one malevolent, Dallas had been so credulous, so accepting, Desi almost quit the team right then and there. Judging by the group e-mails shooting back and forth among the team members this week, everyone was excited about Buck's claims. Where was the objectivity? Where was the proof? It disgusted her that Rampart teetered on the verge of turning into one of those freak shows that attributed every squeak, creak and feeling to ghosts.

She peered over Dallas's shoulder at the computer screen. John Ringo sat on Dallas's right. Pippin O'Malley sat in the chair to the left. All stared at the lines of spikes and waves on the screen.

"Play it again," Pippin demanded. She pushed red curls off her forehead and she flashed a big grin at Desi.

Dallas touched the keyboard. Through the speakers Desi's voice said, "Did you see that? It lit up." A long pause, then "Can you make the lights go on again?" Childish laughter rang out, loud and clear. Dallas looped the recording, isolating the laughter. The laugh was so clear it could have been recorded on any playground.

"That gives me chills," Pippin said. She scrubbed her upper arms with both hands.

Dallas looked over his shoulder at Desi. "What do you think? A ghost?"

All eyes on her, Desi straightened. After she and Buck lost every bit of battery power in the master bedroom, and even the IR camera cut out, Buck had turned on her. Her feelings still stung at his switch from nice guy to stern cop, chastising her about doing something so stupid as to invite a ghost to follow her home.

It *was* stupid. She'd been so caught up in the moment, so fascinated by the apparent responses on the K2 meter, the invitation had slipped out of her mouth without a single thought behind it. The lingering sting turned into fresh anger. Just because Buck Walker believed he had an in with the spirit world didn't mean he had any right to tell her what to do.

He had no right to wreck Rampart with his woo-woo crap.

"It's outside noise," Desi said. "The old coal chute in the furnace room lets in outside noise and it goes straight up that heating vent to the bathroom. There could have been kids playing in the house next door. Or it might have been a television."

"It was responding to questions through the K2," Pippin reminded her.

"My mistake for not rechecking power outlets for power surges."

Dallas and Ringo laughed. Dallas said, "That's why we love ya, kid. Always standing by with a wet blanket. That laugh sounds like it's right up against the recorder. You and Buck didn't hear it. You heard me and Ringo through the vent. You should have heard that laugh."

Desi's cheeks warmed. She still had goose bumps from listening to the childish laughter on the recording. "The jury is still out. We didn't get anything else?"

Ringo made a disgusted noise. "Dallas and I heard footsteps, but none of the recorders picked it up. We've got nothing else."

"Something drained the batteries," Dallas said. "Something used the K2 to communicate. Alec is coming down this week. We're going to do a blessing and help the Moores take back their house."

Desi could have groaned. Alejandro Viho, whom everybody called Alec, was a Cheyenne shaman from Wyoming. He didn't make any claims about psychic powers, but he had enough woo-woo weirdness that Desi always felt uneasy around him. House blessings and casting out spirits were Alec's specialty. Rampart never charged clients for investigations or interventions. The group had genuinely helped people who were disturbed by what they believed was happening in their homes or businesses. Even so, Alec's chanting, drumming and burning sage gave Desi the willies. It seemed to her that clearing rituals crossed the line from scientific research into the occult and superstitious.

"It sure freaked out Buck," Ringo said.

Desi went rigid. Nobody chewed her out and got away with it. *Nobody*. Dallas could pick somebody else to train that jackass in investigation techniques.

"The problem with the Moore house isn't paranormal," Desi said. "They're being poisoned by all the mold and chemicals. The high EMFs could be messing with their heads, too. The house is toxic."

"Can't argue there. I already recommended they move out until the place is cleaned up." Dallas pursed his lips as if to whistle. "That's a great EVP, though. One of the best I've ever heard. Tara is still plugging away with the research. We're hoping it corroborates the K2 session."

Pippin looked at her wristwatch. "I have to scoot. I'll see you guys on Thursday. Great job, Desi. That's an incredible EVP." She reached for the door and paused. "Hey, Desi, walk out with me. I want to ask you something."

Desi picked up her coat and purse. Even though Pippin had been married and widowed, and had had a child, while Desi was single, they'd connected the first time they met. Desi considered the redhead one of her best friends. Something about Pippin's somber expression now made Desi wary.

She followed Pippin outside. "What's up?"

Pippin stopped on the sidewalk and shoved her

hands in her coat pockets. "What happened between you and Buck at the Moore house?"

Desi slung her purse over her shoulder. Her cheeks ached with the cold. "What are you talking about?"

Pippin rolled her eyes and sighed. "Look, it's one thing to thoughtfully examine evidence and look for logical explanations. Have to say, you're the best when it comes to debunking. But now you're angry. Why?"

"I'm not angry."

"Bull. You haven't said a word in the chat room or responded to any of the group e-mails all week." She pointed at the duplex Dallas owned. He lived in one apartment, and the other served as the Rocky Mountain Paranormal Research Team's headquarters. "Every time Buck's name came up you looked ready to hit somebody. I know how you feel about psychics. Everybody knows how you feel. But it doesn't explain why you're so pissed off."

"He just…rubs me the wrong way." She blew a plume of white breath. "I can't believe how everybody is acting like he's the Second Coming! Just because he says he can see ghosts doesn't mean he can." She wanted to tell Pippin about Buck yelling at her and calling her stupid, but that would sound whiney and she was not a whiner. Far more important was the damage he could do to Rampart.

Pippin lowered her voice as if someone might overhear. "I've seen what he can do. Dallas checked him out. I can't explain what I saw, but I know it's real."

It stung that Pippin knew something she didn't. "What did he do?"

Pippin shook her head. "You'll have to ask Dallas. It's kind of personal." She laid a hand on Desi's shoulder and looked her straight in the eye. "Give Buck a chance, okay? He's a really nice man." She grinned and her green eyes sparkled impishly. "Pretty easy on the eyes, too. He's single, and I don't think he has a girlfriend."

Desi groaned, but she smiled, too.

"If Buck is a fake, Dallas will figure it out."

"I know," Desi said.

"So stop being angry." She tapped Desi's forehead. "It gives you wrinkles."

"Fine. I'll be nice." She gave her a friend a quick hug. "But if we find out Buck is running a scam on us, he won't have to worry about Dallas. He'll have to worry about me."

"I WISH YOU'D LET ME go to the meeting," Gwen Hollyhock said wistfully.

Desi looked up from the computer screen in the back room of Hollyhock Antiques and Oddities. Clutching a stack of vintage magazines, her younger sister smiled hopefully. Bangles and charm bracelets jingled with her every movement. While Desi worked on the bookkeeping, Gwen was organizing merchandise, which for her consisted of shifting piles of stuff around. It took a few seconds for Desi's mind to switch from reconciling accounts to realizing Gwen was talking about Rampart's monthly team meeting.

Desi had refused to tell Gwen anything about the Moore house investigation. Dallas hadn't yet published their findings on the public section of the Rampart Web site, so Gwen hadn't been able to hear the EVP of the child's laughter.

"I want to hear what you found in that old house. Every time I drive past it, I get a chill," Gwen said. "I know you found something. You wouldn't avoid me if it turned out to be creaky timbers or squirrels in the walls."

Desi silently cursed Dallas, knowing he'd told Gwen about the Moore house. Desi had asked him countless times to not indulge Gwen's morbid fascination with the paranormal. She had pleaded with him to keep his mouth shut. Gwen was the reason Desi had begun researching the paranormal in the first place. A man, however, would have to be deaf, blind and in a coma to resist Gwen's charms. Dallas Stone was none of those.

"The meetings are members only," she said.

She thought again of her "conversation" via the K2 meter and the EVP of child's laughter. A chill crept from the small of her back, up her spine and to her skull. Nobody knew what caused electronic voice phenomena. There were great recordings collected by researchers all over the world, but thus far only hard-core believers and nuts claimed they were actually the voices of the dead.

"Besides, we didn't find anything. The home-owners are sick. Physically sick. They've torn out walls, exposing mold, and there's dust everywhere. The electrical is a mess. They're stripping woodwork with toxic chemicals. Dallas told them to move out until they finish the renovations. Otherwise, they could end up with permanent health problems."

She wondered how the blessing and casting-out ceremony went today. The Moores would be impressed, no doubt.

Gwen rolled her eyes. "I bet it *is* haunted."

"You think everything is haunted."

Gwen said, "Pfft. I'm looking forward to the day when you run across something you can't explain."

She wandered out of the back room.

Desi returned to the spreadsheet on the computer screen. January had been a slow month, and sales barely covered the store rent. Gwen made most of her money selling "haunted" objects on her Web site. It always appalled Desi how willing people were to plunk down money to own a piece of antique jewelry or a tattered old book reputed to harbor a ghost. What bothered Desi most was Gwen's genuine belief that her treasures were haunted. It didn't help that since Dallas had built Gwen's Web site and maintained it the pair of them talked frequently.

At least Dallas had convinced Gwen to stop holding séances, playing with the Ouija board or otherwise attempting to summon spirits. For that Desi was deeply grateful.

She picked up a pile of envelopes. An overdue notice caught her attention. "Gwen!" She opened the notice, which was from the electric company.

Gwen peered warily around the doorway. "What?"

Desi waved the bill. "Do I have to start writing the checks, too?"

Gwen's cheeks reddened. "I meant to tell you. I kind of overspent at the auction. And after I made a deposit, I sort of forgot about the bill."

Desi glanced between the balance due and the figures on the screen. "There isn't enough to cover it."

Gwen sidled into the room, her skirt swaying and jewelry clinking. She had the decency to look embarrassed. "Could you help a girl out? I'll pay you back. You know I will."

Sure you will, Desi thought with a sigh. She hadn't taken a payment for bookkeeping services from Gwen in over four months, and she no longer bothered keeping track of how much her sister owed her for these little loans.

The sisters had inherited small fortunes from their parents and grandmother. While Desi invested carefully and lived frugally, Gwen burned through her money as if she couldn't get rid of it fast enough. Most of Gwen's inheritance had gone to phony psychics.

"Fine." The bell over the front door rang. "Go sell something. I'll take care of this mess."

Gwen turned away then stopped short. She spun around, dazzling Desi with a smile. "Quick," she whispered. "Get over here so I can punch you in the face!"

"What?"

Gwen held up her hands, wrists together. "I want to get arrested."

Chuckling over her sister's goofiness, Desi went to the doorway and peered out. A police officer studied an antique player piano. He played his long fingers over the yellowed keys, not quite touching the ivory.

"God," Gwen breathed. "Uniforms turn me on. He's so cute!"

Desi's heart leapt into her throat. *No!* No woo-woo freaks around Gwen.

She pushed past Gwen and marched up to the cop. She cleared her throat. "What the hell are you doing here?" She noticed his badge number was 333. Only half-evil, then. What a relief.

Officer Buck Walker stepped away from the piano. The aisle between the collection of old furniture and cabinets full of glassware and collectibles was narrow. He didn't back up, so Desi did. She planted her fists on her hips.

"Hi," he said, flashing her a smile.

Desi felt her sister crowding her.

"Hi," Gwen said. "May I help you? With…anything?"

Buck focused his smile over Desi's head. A sinking sensation weighted Desi. Guys adored Gwen. Even as a little girl with blond hair and big blue eyes, the boys had loved her. She'd left a trail of broken hearts that stretched back to second grade.

The longer Buck smiled at Gwen, the worse Desi felt. It was always like this. Gwen shined; Desi turned invisible. Her golden sister's dark little shadow.

"I'm Buck Walker," he said.

"Oh!" Gwen stretched an elegant hand, sparkling with rings on every finger, over Desi's shoulder. "The new guy. I'm Gwen, Desi's little sister." They shook hands. Gwen squeezed Desi to the side and draped a companionable arm over her shoulders.

Desi clenched her teeth. Gwen did it on purpose, emphasizing that Gwen inherited all the tall, leggy genes and Desi was a shrimp. When Buck turned his attention and those warm, brown eyes back to Desi, a little ping in her belly caught her off guard.

"It's my day off," Buck said. He glanced down at his uniform. "But I had to go to court this morning. Since I was in the neighborhood, I thought I'd drop in and say hi. Maybe go for some coffee?"

In the first place, Buck shouldn't have known her sister owned this antique store. In the second place, he sounded pretty damned certain Desi would be here. Which was ridiculous. She was a freelance bookkeeper with clients all over town, and she only visited this store a few days a month. In the third place, if he thought for a moment she'd forgotten the way he'd dressed her down for extending an invitation to a ghost, he was as nutty as Gwen and the two of them deserved each other.

Gwen dropped her arm and waggled her fingers for Buck to step aside. He did so, barely giving her a glance as she sauntered past. "Go have coffee, sweetie. You've been working all morning without a break. You need some fresh air."

"I don't have time," Desi said, hating the sullen tone in her voice. "I have another client in an hour."

Buck's smile faded. He continued to stare at her. A searching stare that grew in intensity, his eyes growing darker, drawing her in.

Desi looked away first. She lowered her voice. "What are you really doing here?"

He drew his head aside. "Are you mad at me?"

"Hell yes! I don't appreciate some new guy waltzing in and yelling at me. You have no right to treat me like a dumb kid."

"Are you talking about the K2 meter? I didn't yell at you."

"You did. And it was uncalled for."

He leaned in close, but she stood her ground. His uniform didn't intimidate her and neither did his size. "Whether you believe it or not, a Dark Presence haunts that house. Inviting it into your life was stupid."

"So now I'm stupid?"

"I didn't say that. I'm concerned. I need to know that thing didn't follow you."

It astonished her that the city of Colorado Springs gave this guy a gun. He was insane. "Take your concern and march it out of here, Officer. I have work to do."

He straightened his broad shoulders. He wore a bulletproof vest under his uniform shirt and it made his chest look bigger. He looked beyond her and a faint frown lowered his brows. His face relaxed and the corners of his mouth twitched. "Have it your way. See you at the meeting tonight."

She lifted a shoulder. "You don't have to be there. It's just shop talk."

A tight grin turned his face from handsome to dangerously handsome. "Dallas told me meetings are mandatory if I want to stay on the team." He raised a hand as if tipping a hat, turned around and walked away.

Desi's cheeks burned.

"Very nice meeting you, Gwen," he said.

"Same here, Buck. Don't be a stranger. Come on back anytime."

Gwen waited until the door closed behind Buck before she let loose a merry laugh. "OMG!" she exclaimed. "That's the guy you called a pinhead jerk? Why don't you two just get a room and, you know, duke it out."

The burn spread across Desi's entire face and neck. "What are you talking about?"

"You." Gwen laughed and the music of it filled the store. "That guy really likes you. I saw the look on his face. And then you? Oh my God, Desdemona Hollyhock! If you got any hotter, you'd set the joint on fire."

"That is the stupidest thing I have ever heard, Gwendolyn Marie Hollyhock. Buck is a jackass and I can't stand him."

Gwen dismissed that comment with a flip of her hand. "I might not be able to balance a checkbook, sweetie, but I can spot true love from a mile away."

Desi spun about and marched into the back room. She'd be having tea and cookies with Casper the Friendly Ghost before she ever had a romantic thought about Buck Walker.

BUCK SLID behind the wheel and slammed the door. Who did that imperious little twit think she was, anyway? Standing there in that tight red sweater with her boobs half hanging out, acting like he'd committed a crime. Fine, she didn't believe he saw spirits. Didn't believe he communicated with them. He jammed a key at the ignition, then twisted and pushed on it for a few seconds before realizing it was the wrong key. He fumbled the right key around on the ring and started the Jeep.

He glared at the storefront of Hollyhock Antiques and Oddities. The windows were filled with claw-footed furniture, antique dolls and stacks of old china. He couldn't see inside, but he could picture Desi with her fall of sleek, sable hair and those blue eyes snapping with anger. Her attitude didn't belong in the field of paranormal research. Skepticism might be healthy, but she carried it to a ridiculous extreme.

"You're ridiculous," he snarled at the storefront. "You're not that cute, either."

He checked the street and backed out of the parking space.

At least he'd seen no sign of the Dark Presence. Sensed no malevolence surrounding her or lurking in the corners.

A chuckle rose and anger faded. Desi Hollyhock was *damned* cute. He shook his head, amused at himself for letting her get his goat. He had the temperament and training to stay coolheaded under any circumstances. He'd be damned if he was going to let some pint-sized girl in a sexy sweater and tight jeans get to him.

Too bad she was unaware of the friendly spirit he'd glimpsed accompanying her. Guardian spirits, he called them. Such spirits seemed to have unfinished business or they clung to living loved ones who were troubled. Desi Hollyhock didn't appear troubled. She was just a pill.

He looked forward to the Rocky Mountain Paranormal Research Team meeting tonight. She might be a tough cookie, but he was tougher.

If she wore that red sweater, all the better for him.

Chapter Three

When Buck entered Rampart headquarters it was as if a magnet drew his eyes to Desi Hollyhock. She was seated at a battered conference table that took up much of the meeting room. She wore the red sweater, and the swell of her soft breasts seemed to glow. Desi glanced up when he walked inside, but immediately returned to her conversation with a tall, brown-haired woman.

Dallas Stone beckoned Buck. Peeling out of his coat, Buck joined him in the kitchen. Dallas shook Buck's hand then indicated a man.

"Alec Viho, Buck Walker."

They shook hands. As soon as Buck made contact he felt a shock of recognition. Alec looked to be in his mid-thirties with long, black hair tied back in a ponytail. His face was dark, hard-planed, with a jutting nose, prominent cheekbones and a sharply outlined jaw. Buck knew they hadn't met, but something about Alec struck a chord.

Maybe it was the aura.

Buck had seen glimmers of color surrounding people before. It hadn't happened often and he'd never figured out why only some people had them. Alec's aura was green and soothing.

"Glad to you meet you," Alec said. "Dallas says good things."

"Grab a drink," Dallas said. "I'm going to see if I can wrangle that herd of cats into a meeting."

Buck pulled a soda from the fridge. He felt Alec studying him.

"So you have a direct line to the dead," Alec said. He spoke with the same casualness as if he'd said, "So I see you drive a Jeep."

Maybe it was the aura, or maybe the man's utter calm, but Buck felt a sense of relief. "I guess," Buck said.

"You're untrained." Alec nodded. "That's okay. Never too late to learn."

"Do you see ghosts?"

"Not so much."

Buck's head reeled. He'd never met anyone so accepting. Alec stared out the glass sliding door. Though it was only six o'clock, the backyard was dead dark. Buck could just make out the bulky shape of a gas barbecue grill and a basketball hoop mounted on a tall pole. Buck asked, "Why do you believe me?"

"Is there a reason I shouldn't?"

Feminine laughter caused both men to turn their heads. The female members of the team had gathered at the far end of the conference table. Buck caught Desi's eyes. She gave him an icy look before turning back to her friends.

Alec chuckled, low and charged with amusement. "Don't take it personal, Buck. She doesn't like me, either."

Buck stiffened, wondering if his feelings were that transparent or if Alec was extremely intuitive. He hoped it was the latter. "She's a piece of work."

"She has a good heart. A warrior's heart. But she shoulders the problems of others instead of looking at her own." Alec smiled. "She throws boulders on her own life path."

Interesting man, Buck thought. "Did you get to the Moore house today?"

Alec nodded. "It was quiet when we left. All are where they belong now."

Buck hoped the little boy had joined his loved ones on the Other Side. He really hoped the Dark Presence had gone straight to hell.

"Everybody's here," Dallas said. "Let's get the show on the road."

Buck took a chair near the head of the table and Alec sat beside him. Fifteen people crowded around the conference table. Dallas pointed to Tara Chase, Rampart's researcher and historian.

Tara opened a folder. "I found more info about the Moore house. You've all seen the transcript of the question-and-answer session with Desi, Buck and the K2 meter, right? If you didn't get the e-mail, let me know and I'll resend it." She glanced at her notes. "After the original owner died, his younger brother inherited the house. He had six children. Three boys and three girls. The youngest, a little boy named Jonathon, was the only child of the husband's third wife. He died of influenza in 1919. He was nine years old."

"Wow," John Ringo said. "That fits exactly with what Buck and Desi picked up in the K2 session. Good job, Tara."

She closed the folder. "I should be able to post all the material I found out about the house this week. Even without ghosts it's a fascinating place."

Dallas nodded. "We did a blessing at the Moores today. It went well. The Moores aren't leaving, but they did move their bedroom downstairs to a room where nothing is torn up. They say they feel better since the investigation, and they haven't been seeing or hearing things. I think Mr. Moore was more shaken up by the EVP than Mrs. Moore was, but he seems cool with it now. Especially since his wife isn't waking up screaming anymore. They invited us to come back when the renovations are finished to see if we can catch anything else. Chalk one up to the good guys."

Heads bobbed and murmurs rippled through the room. Buck caught Desi's sideways glance. She slid her attention away as if she hadn't been looking at him at all.

"Well, folks," Pippin O'Malley said. The pretty

redhead with big green eyes and a smattering of freckles tapped the scarred tabletop with her knuckles. "I have a case our resident psychic might be able to help with."

All eyes turned to Buck and his spine went rigid.

"I've been talking to a single mom with two kids. Her cousin lives with her. The cousin says she's a psychic and she senses unhealthy spirits in the house. Our single mom thinks her children are in danger."

"Boot the cousin to the street," Desi said. "Problem solved."

"I agree," Pippin said. "But I don't think she'll do that."

"Any activity?" Dallas asked.

"Only the cousin's claims. I feel bad for the mom. She's barely making it financially, but she's ready to break her lease and move her kids out."

Buck asked, "How do you think I could help?"

Pippin smiled at Buck. "A psychic reading."

Several people burst into laughter. Buck felt like slinking out of the meeting and never returning.

"Shut up!" Dallas rapped the table. "Come on, guys. We aren't icy-cold scientists. Part of our mission is to help people. For God's sake, we're talking little kids here. Go ahead, Pip."

Buck hated the word "reading" It sounded like something you did with a 1-900 number after asking a sucker for a credit card number.

Pippin said, "Buck isn't like those guys on tele-vision."

Desi snorted and slumped on her chair. "They're all crackpots." The hard look she tossed at Buck said *Just like you*.

Buck met her glare with narrowed eyes.

"I'm ninety-nine percent certain there's nothing paranormal going on," Pippin said. "So let's call this a mission of mercy. We do a full investigation, then Buck can do a reading. Counteract the cousin. Who *does* sound like one of those guys on television, by the way."

"A battle of the psychics?" Desi shook her head, sending her hair swinging across her shoulders. "Pip, I'm sorry, but that's just dumb." She looked around the room. "Doesn't anybody else see how dangerous that could be? The cousin is an attention junkie. You all know how people like that are. The more we expose her as a fake, the harder she'll try to prove us wrong."

A few agreed, others disagreed, but Buck stayed silent. Desi made a good point.

Pippin said, "Speaking as a therapist *and* as a single mom, I think she's looking for someone to assure her the kids are safe. Maybe a few sessions with me can help her work out the issues with her cousin. It will help if an investigation fails to catch anything."

"It'll make us a laughing stock," Desi said. "Psychic crap undermines our credibility."

Buck's jaw tightened. "It's not crap. The things I see and hear are real. What it is exactly and where it comes from is a mystery. But that doesn't mean I'm a fake." Temptation burned to tell her that right now, right in this room, several spirits were hanging around—including the entity he'd noticed near Desi at the antique store.

"There's an explanation for hearing voices. Schizophrenia."

"There's an explanation for *you*," he shot back. "Close-minded."

"I'm not watching you play 'Oooh, I'm picking up a J name.' John, Jack?" She pitched her voice high. "A friend of my third cousin, twice removed, is named Julie! That's it! Oh yay! You really are psychic!" She clapped her hands in mock delight.

Buck's jaw ached from tension. This made twice in one day Desi had poked his temper.

Dallas's eyes blazed and his big hands clenched, making veins stand out on the backs. "Drop this for now, Pip. You can fill me in on the details later."

The meeting resumed on a subdued note. After Dallas announced it was over, some of the team members looked as if they couldn't escape quickly enough.

Buck pulled on his coat. He and Desi were going to have this out, one way or another.

"HEY, DESI," Dallas said. "Stick around a minute."

She watched Buck leave the house. The anxious ache in her belly worsened. She couldn't believe how she'd acted. She couldn't believe she'd been so nasty…so childish. Drawing a steadying breath, she faced Dallas Stone.

She stared over his head at a framed poster for the movie *Swamp Thing*.

Ringo kept his head down and his hands busy clearing the table and straightening chairs. Dallas crooked a finger, indicating Desi should join him in the kitchen. He rested his backside against a counter and folded his arms over his chest. "What the hell is going on between you and Buck?"

"Nothing."

"Yeah, right. Whether you like it or not, I'm convinced he's the real thing. He's as interested in finding the truth as any other member of the team. I'm a skeptic when it comes to claims by psychics and mediums, too. You know damned good and well that I would never invite anyone to join unless I thought they were serious."

"I have a lot going on with work, and I'm stressed out. I—I didn't mean it."

"The problem is," Dallas said, "you did mean it. I'm not having any dissension on the team. We don't need negative energy."

Desi wished she could curl into a tiny ball and disappear. Her throat tightened. She admired and respected Dallas as much or more than any other man she knew. His disappointment in her hurt worse than if he'd slapped her across the face.

"I won't put you and Buck on the same investigations. I expect you to ease up at the meetings, okay?"

"Okay."

She slunk out of the duplex.

At home, she took a moment to breathe in the air of her little town house. This was her sanctuary. She turned on her computer. She had work to do for a client and she looked forward to it. Numbers were rational. Numbers never changed their character or delved into the unexplained. Numbers always made sense.

"Get off my chair, Spike," she said.

The yellow tomcat twitched an ear. She picked him up and he rumbled and meowed in protest. "Go sleep in your basket, you big grouch. That's my chair. I don't know why we have to have this argument every single time I need to use the computer."

Her cell phone rang and she glanced at the clock. Good news never came at this time of night. She answered warily, "Hello?"

"Hi, Desi. This is Buck. Sorry for calling so late."

Fresh humiliation rolled through her. "Hi."

"I can't sleep unless I apologize for tonight. I'm really sorry."

She lifted her eyebrows. She caught a movement from the corner of her eye and turned in time to see Spike hop back up on her desk chair.

"Desi?"

An apology to him caught in her throat. "I'm not sure what to say."

"How about saying we can start over. We got off on the wrong foot. I'd like to keep working with you. I can learn a lot."

He came across as so genuine he was hard to resist. His voice was seductive in its sincerity. She pictured him in the olive-green sweater he'd worn tonight, stretched over his shoulders and chest. As Pippin had said, he was very easy on the eyes. Probably a nice guy, too. She supposed as long as he didn't offer to read her palm or start talking in tongues she could tolerate him.

As for the psychic abilities, well, she thought, a researcher *should* wait until all the data was in. "Thanks. I do act stupid sometimes. We can start over."

A bright flash in the kitchen was followed by a loud *pop*. She squeaked.

"Desi?"

She laughed. "A lightbulb just blew. It startled me. But never mind. Thank you for calling, Buck. I appreciate it. It's big of you."

"Maybe—" He paused. "Good. So I'll see you around."

After she hung up, she put the cell phone on the charger. She scooped up the cat. Spike grumbled and tensed as she snuggled him. She rubbed between his ears. He acted like a little kid suffering smoochies from an overly enthusiastic auntie. "Everybody else likes him. Guess it's only fair to wait until he actually screws up before I jump down his throat."

Another lightbulb blew. Spike twisted. His claws hooked into her arm and she yelped, dropping him.

"Damn it!" She glared past the breakfast bar into the now-dim kitchen. She winced at the scratches where beads of blood formed on her skin. Shaking her head in disgust, she went upstairs to find the antiseptic.

UNSETTLED, BUCK FROWNED at the phone. On the one hand he was relieved to have made up with Desi. On the other hand, a most unpleasant sensation prickled his scalp. He'd felt something when she said the lightbulb blew. A brief feeling, a microinstant of *knowing*. Sourness filled his mouth and settled in his guts.

Alec said the Moore house was cleansed of spirit activity. Even so… The prickling worsened, and Buck dragged in a deep breath.

Dark Presences. After his encounter with their malignancy in the past, Buck had vowed to never allow one to notice him again. Like all ghosts, Dark Presences had unfinished business and they had an eternity to finish it. Unlike most other ghosts, Dark Presences had the power to manipulate the physical world. They had the power to manipulate people.

Whether she meant it as a joke or not, Buck feared Desi had opened a doorway to something very bad.

SQUINTING AGAINST SUNLIGHT, Desi grabbed the obnoxiously ringing cell phone. If Gwen was calling at this ungodly hour of the morning, Desi was going to strangle her over the airwaves. In case it was a business call, Desi forced brightness into her tone. "Hello?"

"Hi, Desi. This is Buck. Sorry to wake you."

It struck her that he sounded certain he'd reached her. He'd done that last night, too. She glanced at the clock. It was barely noon.

"I wasn't sleeping."

"I can call back later."

"It's okay. What can I do for you?" She pushed Spike off her foot. He gave her the stink eye then headed back to sleep. She stretched and rolled her shoulders, the headed downstairs for coffee.

"I wanted to ask you about Kirlian photography. It takes pictures of auras."

She started to make coffee. "It's bunk. All it takes pictures of are water molecules reacting to an electrical charge." She scooped an extra spoonful of coffee into the filter. She hadn't gone to bed until five this morning. "Dallas has collected a lot of research about auras and aural photography. Anything you want to know about the subject is on the Web site." She started the coffee brewing and yawned. "Why are you asking about Kirlian photography?"

"I caught part of a TV show about psychic healers. It mentioned Kirlian and I was wondering about it."

There were millions of Web sites on the Internet with information about aural photography. Buck didn't need to ask her about it. She had to admit it was much nicer to wake up to Buck's warm voice than it was to hear about her sister's latest haunted treasure or to get a call from a panicky client with lost receipts or a bounced check.

"I'd look it up on the Internet," he said, "but my laptop is an antique and the connection is so slow it drives me crazy."

She opened the pantry door and studied the contents.

"Or I'd go to the library, but I'm working. Do you mind me asking questions?"

A crash made her jump and she almost dropped the phone. At the sight of the coffee can on the floor and coffee spilled everywhere her jaw dropped. "That damned cat!"

"What happened?"

"Spike just knocked a whole can of coffee on the floor. I hate that cat sometimes." She stood on tiptoe, trying to see over the breakfast counter. Spike had disappeared. The coward. "I have to clean up this mess. I'll talk to you later."

"Okay." He sounded uncertain. "Later."

She set the phone on the counter and cursing the cat, began sweeping up the mess. She'd opened the can only two days ago. Ten dollars down the drain. Spike was darned lucky she'd already started a pot brewing, or he'd have to face her caffeine-deprived wrath.

By the time she had the kitchen floor cleaned, Spike still hadn't shown up. Usually he took great pleasure in watching her clean up his messes. She began to worry that maybe the coffee can had struck him and he was hurt. She went looking for him.

Sound asleep, Spike lay curled in the same spot he'd been in when she got out of bed.

BUCK PARKED THE PATROL CAR in the space next to the little red Subaru. He got out and watched Desi crossing the parking lot. She lugged a box of paper. She frowned at his approach, but willingly allowed him to take the heavy box. She pointed a remote at the Subaru and popped open the trunk. She looked him up and down, taking in the uniform.

"What are you doing here?" she asked, and stepped aside so he could put the box in the trunk.

He pointed at Garden of the Gods Road. "This is my beat. I made my quota of speeding tickets, so thought I'd take a break and say hi."

He sensed a shimmer of energy around Desi. The entity felt female, motherly, and he got the distinct impression she noticed him. It would be easy to make contact. Easy that is, if the entity weren't attached to Desi Hollyhock.

"How…?" She looked around the parking lot of the office supply store. "How did you know I'd be here?"

He'd stopped worrying about the source of his *knowing* a long time ago. "I was cutting through the parking lot and saw you come out of the store."

She closed the trunk, her face wary. "And you just happened to park right next to my car?"

He shrugged. He listened to a call from dispatch coming through the radio earpiece. Nobody needed him. "Your license plate number." He tapped the side of his head. "It's a gift."

"A psychic gift?"

"Only if all cops are psychic. We tend to notice license plates."

She wore a black peacoat and a cream-colored knit cap. Her cheeks were pink with cold and her eyes were bright, the bluest blue he'd ever seen. They rivaled the winter sky. She was so pretty, he could stand here and look at her all day.

"What a coincidence," she said. "Especially since I don't usually shop at this store. They're having a big sale. If you need computer paper, now's the time to get it. Can I ask you a question? What do the people you work with think about your abilities?"

"Do you admit I have abilities?"

She smiled. "No."

"I don't tell them."

She looked surprised. "Huh."

"You don't want to know what cops really think about mediums. Every time there's a big crime, especially a murder or missing child, 911 is flooded with calls from people who've had visions and dreams."

"I see."

"I wish I did. See, that is." He hunched deeper into his coat against the cold. "I figured out I'm a freak a long time ago. Different. I still don't know what it means. I still don't know why me and not everybody. I spent a lot of years trying to hide from it."

He sensed her uncertainty, read it in her expressive eyes.

"I've done some good with it, helped some people. Some bad things have happened, too. Rampart looks like a good opportunity to figure myself out. Maybe if I know what I'm doing, I can do something useful."

"Get your own television show?"

"Ouch."

She folded her arms. In the busy parking lot pedestrians and people in cars stared. A cop and a civilian always drew curiosity.

"Okay," she said. "Just so we're straight. I've run across a lot of so-called psychics, mediums, fortune-tellers, channelers and even a few telepaths. I consider every single one flat-out evil. They exploit the grieving, greedy and just plain dumb. I admit that Rampart has collected some really good evidence about the paranormal. I've seen a lot of things that can't be explained and I'm willing to accept that there may be something out there. What I have never seen is evidence of any type, under any circumstances, that anybody can communicate with the dead."

She was honest about her feelings. He liked that about her.

"Fair enough. So tell me, if I promise to not talk about my adventures with dead relatives, will you go out to dinner with me?"

He liked her open surprise, too.

A call came over the radio. Dispatch wanted his location. He thumbed the radio transmitter clipped to his shoulder and responded. A business reported a break-in.

"I have to go. I'll call you."

"Okay."

As he pulled out of the parking lot he watched her. With her head cocked and wearing a bemused smile, she watched him. She definitely liked him, even if she didn't realize it yet. Sometimes, he thought with a chuckle, *knowing* things came in handy.

Chapter Four

Wishing her town house had an attached garage, Desi lugged the heavy box of paper toward her house. At least, the weather had been dry and she didn't have to fight ice and snow piles to get from her car to the front door.

Her next-door neighbor came outside, spotted Desi and made a small sound of surprise.

"Hi, Annaliese," Desi said. "Could you help a girl out and unlock my door?"

"You have been out?" the older German woman asked.

Desi shifted her grip. The sun was blindingly bright, but the temperature was about twenty degrees and her hands were ice. "Yeah, and I'm about to drop this box." She moved so Annaliese could take the keys clipped to her purse.

"Well!" Annaliese hurried to unlock Desi's door. The concrete porch was too small for more than one person at a time. Instead of letting Desi enter, Annaliese stood there and frowned.

Desi adored her neighbor, but the box was growing heavier by the second. "Go on in," Desi said, and put a foot on the concrete step. "Please."

Annaliese shook a finger. "I thought you were home. I was coming to tell you to turn down the television. It is so loud!"

"I never leave the TV on."

"Oh, yes, you are such a good neighbor. Never any noise or parties." She clamped her hands over her ears and swayed side to side. "Oh, oh, oh! My walls are shaking."

Now Desi realized the noisy television she assumed came from another town house in the row actually came from her house. "Let me in. Go. I'm about to drop this on my foot."

Annaliese went inside and held the door for Desi. Sure enough, her television blared at full volume. Desi put the box on the floor, dropped her purse and rushed to turn it off. The silence was instant and blessed. She stuck her freezing hands under her armpits and turned to her neighbor.

Annaliese smiled, showing very white teeth. "This is so unlike you, Desi."

The television remote lay on the coffee table. *Spike.* Desi couldn't remember if she'd been watching the news before she left to run her errands. If she had forgotten to turn off the TV, and the cat walked on or sat on the remote, he could have pressed the volume control.

"It won't happen again," Desi said. "I promise."

Annaliese blew air between her teeth. "I believe you. All done now. You must promise to come over later. It is so cold I have to bake. I am making olive bread. Old, old family recipe from Germany."

Annaliese loved to bake, but she always claimed an excuse for it—it was a holiday, or somebody's birthday, or it was raining. She even said once that it was so miserably hot she might as well make cookies to justify the heat.

"I can't wait," Desi said. "I'm sorry about the noise. It will not happen again."

Desi followed the older woman out, returning to her car to collect the rest of her bags. It was definitely possible Spike had turned up the volume on the TV. The more Desi thought about it, however, the more positive she felt that she had not left the TV on in the first place.

After carrying the rest of the bags inside, she called, "Spike? Here, kitty. Where are you, bad boy?"

A meow answered. She looked around and heard paws pattering frantically against the basement door. She opened it and the cat sauntered out, his tail flipping in annoyance about being locked in the basement.

Desi sang along to the golden oldies radio station as she keyed numbers into a spreadsheet. Piles of receipts were spread across her desk. She'd spent an hour organizing scraps of paper for her client.

She liked Joe. He always fed her a big plate of his special lasagna whenever she visited his Italian bistro downtown. She hated his habit of filling a paper sack with receipts without making the slightest effort to sort them by type or date. He was almost as bad as her sister. But at least she didn't have to scour his restaurant to find mislaid papers the way she had to at the antique store.

Spike jumped onto the desk. She picked him up, again, and set him on the floor. He stretched against her leg, unsheathing his claws. "Ow!" She shoved him away. He sat and glared at her, tail twitching. "What do you want? You're driving me crazy this morning. I already fed you." As soon as she began typing, he stretched against her leg again. His claws pricked through her jeans. "Ow! That's it!" He tried to run, but she caught him, tossed him onto the basement stairs and closed the door. "Cat jail for you."

The phone rang then, so she settled back in front of the computer and answered.

It was Gwen. "Guess what?"

"I'm busy, Gwen."

"You're always busy. But you'll never guess who I ran into at Chico's."

"Paul Newman." Desi peered closely at an invoice. The printer ink had been low and the numbers were only partially printed.

"Didn't you hear? He passed away months ago. I saw your cute cop friend."

A ripple ran through Desi's chest and belly. Buck had called but, uncertain if she wanted to go out with him, she'd let it go to voice mail. She hadn't listened to his message yet. What if he ate with his fingers or flirted with servers or was a lousy tipper?

"The girls and I stopped in for nachos and a beer. There he was. He's even cuter out of uniform. He was with a friend. Will. Have you met him?"

A most unpleasant image of beautiful Gwen chatting it up and laughing with Buck formed in Desi's head. Buck drowning in Gwen's eyes, and sneaking glimpses of her ample breasts while she charmed him into following her to the ends of the earth and slaying a few dragons along the way.

"Buck and I don't have a personal relationship," she said. "I don't know his friends."

"You should. Will's a hoot. He had me laughing so hard I almost peed my pants."

The scene in Desi's head shifted to the Mexican restaurant with its cozy booths and dim lighting. The girls, as Gwen called them, were her two best friends. The Three Blonde-keteers, Grandma used to call them when they were in high school. In her mental scenario they charmed Buck and his friend with intimate conversation and lots of flirting.

"I really am busy, Gwen. Let me call you later."

"Buck asked about you."

"He did?" She winced at the eager squeak that came out of her mouth.

"He wanted to know what you do for fun. I told him you're a total stick in the mud, but you like to hike. Turns out he hikes, too. He likes you, sweetie."

Warmth replaced the sourness in her stomach. She went into the kitchen to make a fresh cup of tea. "I barely know him," Desi said. She studied boxes of herbal teas. She bet Buck would be an excellent companion on a mountain trail. He wasn't the type to run his mouth and make a lot of noise, and he sure wouldn't have any trouble keeping up no matter how tough the trail.

"The girls and I voted," Gwen said. "You two are meant for each other. It's unanimous."

Laughing, Desi selected blackberry tea, filled the cup with water and put it in the microwave.

"Don't laugh," Gwen said. "When's the last time you had a boyfriend? Or even a date? Maybe a little…*sugar* would loosen you up."

Gwen didn't get it. Gwen never lacked for male companionship. Sometimes she had three or four men vying for the chance to take her out for dinner and dancing. But Desi was a loser magnet. She could easily imagine Buck Walker as a buddy, but as a boyfriend? He could have any woman he wanted. Not even Gwen was out of his league.

The microwave dinged. "I have a ton of work to do," Desi said. "I'll call you later."

There was silence on the line, then Gwen said, "Are you okay?"

"I'm fine."

"I was just teasing. I didn't mean to hurt your feelings."

"It's okay, Gwen. Really. I'll call you later. Maybe we can watch a movie or something."

She disconnected but stood for a moment, annoyed at herself for caring what Buck did or did not do. She felt relieved, too, that he'd kept his mouth shut. If he'd mentioned psychic crap to Gwen, then Gwen would have been at her door instead of merely calling.

She set the phone down and pulled the steaming tea from the microwave. Desi held the cup near her nose, hoping for soothing effects. She never got upset about a guy. Sure, she felt lonely sometimes and wished for a little romance. Overall she liked her life. She had a nice house and lots of good friends, and she certainly stayed busy with her work and Rampart. It wasn't like she mooned around, bored and dissatisfied.

She walked past the breakfast bar and stopped short. The cup slipped from suddenly numb fingers. It bounced on the carpet, splashing her jeans with hot tea. Breath lodged in her throat, and her lungs froze.

All the receipts, invoices and other papers that had been on her desk were now scattered across the floor.

DESI CHECKED the caller ID. It was Buck.

This had not been a good day. After cleaning up tea stains, broken china and scattered paper, and unable to blame the cat, since he'd been locked in the basement, she'd wasted over an hour trying to figure out how the papers had blown off her desk. She checked every door and window for drafts. She even climbed onto a chair and held a candle around the ceiling light fixture to see if there was an air leak. All that proved was that holding a burning candle near a popcorn-textured ceiling was dumb. She'd had to clean off soot then vacuum the bits of texture material that fell on the floor. She had turned the furnace fan on and off several times. Nothing on her desk so much as twitched. She'd even flipped through news stations on the radio and television to see if Colorado Springs had experienced any seismic activity. Nerved up, jumping at every little noise, she'd managed to finish the monthly book-keeping for Joe's restaurant, but it had taken twice as long as usual.

On the fourth ring she answered the cell phone.

"Hi, Desi," Buck said. "What's wrong?"

Quit being spooky! "Nothing's wrong."

"Do you know what the guys at work call me? The Human Lie Detector."

Bad enough that apparently a mini-tornado had run through her living room, but now he was going all woo-woo on her. She had chills on top of goose bumps. "Good for you," she sputtered. "I'm busy. I have to go."

"Desi, come on, talk to me. Is something going on in your house? I've been thinking about you all day. I'm worried."

Before she could reply, noise blared from the phone and banged against her eardrum. She cried out and almost dropped the cell phone. The screen flared then went black. Though she thumbed the Power button, the phone merely screeched and popped, and a wisp of blue smoke curled from the casing. She flung the phone away, half expecting it to sprout legs and come after her.

For the very first time since she'd signed the papers making this house her own, she wanted to be anywhere but here.

BUCK REDIALED Desi's number. It went straight to voice mail. He knew for certain she hadn't hung up on him then turned off her phone. The fear he'd heard in her voice rattled him.

He paced aimlessly through his apartment. He picked up a magazine and set it down. He lifted his old Gibson guitar from the stand. He fingered a few chords and played a few notes, but his nerves were as taut as the guitar strings. Not even a rerun of a college football game on ESPN could hold his attention.

Desi needed him.

He pulled on a coat, picked up his keys and cell phone, and left the apartment.

Ghosts rarely harmed people, he knew. A poltergeist might damage household items, and even slap a person or scratch them, but there was not one credibly documented case of a ghost or poltergeist seriously injuring or killing a person.

Dark Presences, on the other hand, operated by different rules. He didn't know if they were ghosts at all or were instead something demonic. They did hurt people. They killed.

He drove across town to Desi's town-house community. He parked in a guest space and got out of the Jeep. He exhaled white clouds. Weather reports predicted snow in the next few days.

An empty parking space drew him. He saw 1411 painted on the asphalt. Desi's space.

He turned to the double row of town houses designed to vaguely resemble Colonial-style row houses. Most of the windows glowed with interior lights and the flickering of television sets. Number 1411 was dark. He rang the doorbell anyway.

The front door of the neighboring house opened, the storm door squeaking. "Do you look for Desi?" a woman with an accent asked. *German,* Buck thought.

"Yes, ma'am." He walked down the steps. "I'm a friend of hers. I tried to call, but she's not answering. I'm a little worried."

The woman emanated a touch of suspicious nervousness, but a lot of friendliness, too. The warm, rich, yeasty aromas drifting from the open door made Buck's belly growl.

The woman flipped her hand. "I tell her, those cell phones are no good. Why do all you young people need to talk, talk, talk all the time? A good black telephone, plugged in the wall, is all you need. You don't answer? Pah! Let them call back if it's so important."

He sensed this woman's loneliness. She held a lot of good will, too. Desi's living guardian spirit. "She had trouble with her phone?"

"It blew up. *Boom!* I tell her, get a good black phone and she won't have problems like that." She laughed. "Poor little thing, had to go buy another. I tell her, buy one tomorrow. No need running around when it so cold." She shook a finger at Buck. "You young people are addicted to your cell phones."

As if on cue his cell phone rang.

The woman cried, "See!" She hooted laughter.

Buck checked the caller ID. It was Dallas Stone. Sheepishly, he mumbled an apology to the woman. She assured him she would let Desi know he'd stopped by, and she withdrew into the warm and fragrant house.

Headed for his Jeep, Buck answered the phone.

Dallas said, "Hey, Buck, are you still free tomorrow?"

He got in the Jeep and started the engine. He knew why Dallas called. The team was working with the single mother with the "sensitive" cousin. "I am. How did the investigation go?"

Dallas grumbled. "Good and bad. We spent eight hours in the house, hitting it with everything we've got."

"Did you catch anything?"

"Only that goofball cousin. Get this. She claims to channel the spirit of Morgan le Fay."

Buck lifted his eyebrows. He'd heard many

mediums claim to channel such historical figures as Cleopatra and Marie Antoinette, but King Arthur's witchy half-sister was a first. "Um, has anyone let her know that's a fictional character?"

"I wish *she* was fictional," Dallas said. "I thought we were going to have to knock her out and tie her up to get her out of the way. Pippin has a good idea what's really going on. The cousin is unemployed. She can't afford her own place, so Joan, our client, lets her cousin live rent-free in exchange for baby-sitting. The cousin wants a bigger house."

"Lofty motives." The Jeep's heater vents began blowing hot air. "Do you still want me to do a reading?"

"Tomorrow morning, nine o'clock, if that works for you. We'll do it at headquarters. That'll guarantee the cousin doesn't interfere. I think meeting a real medium will give Joan the push she needs to stand up to her cousin. Or, better yet, throw her out."

"Sounds good to me." Buck glanced at Desi's empty parking space. "Will Desi be there?"

Dallas snorted a laugh. "Don't need the negative vibes."

"It might give her some perspective about what I do."

"Don't count on it, Buck. She hates psychics."

"I kind of get that impression," Buck said.

"She has a sister—"

"Gwen."

"You've met her?" Dallas sounded surprised.

Buck picked up an undercurrent of jealousy. "She's interesting."

Dallas said, "Yep, that's Gwen. Interesting. She blew through about a quarter of a million dollars on séances and mediums. Almost her entire inheritance. Desi is still righteously pissed off about it."

Before the situation turned ugly at the Moore house, Desi had mentioned she was a bookkeeper. Not exactly the sort of job he'd associate with an heiress. It made Buck wonder if Gwen had somehow blown through Desi's money, too. That would explain a lot of Desi's hostility. "I see."

"I really want you on the team, man," Dallas said. "I'd love to gather hard evidence about what it is you can do. I don't know how to do that yet, but we'll figure it out. In the meantime, it's better if you and Desi don't interfere with each other."

"Makes sense. I'll see you tomorrow at nine." After he ended the call, the car was warm enough that he'd stopped shivering. Desi had lied when she said nothing strange was happening in her house. However, his instincts said—and he always trusted his instincts—pushing Desi Hollyhock's back against a wall was a mistake. He had no choice except to wait for her to come to him.

DESI PARKED HER CAR on the street in front of Dallas's duplex. He had called while she was with a client, and the message he'd left sounded very mysterious. When she finally got him on the phone he'd sounded like a kid at Christmas. All he would tell her was that she needed to get to Rampart headquarters.

John Ringo opened the door before she had a chance to knock. He was a big, bearish man with a full black beard. Usually Desi thought he was a big goof, but at other times she sensed something much deeper about him. He never talked about his personal life. Nobody, except Dallas, seemed to know what he did when he wasn't ghost hunting.

"Baby girl, we are about to rock your world."

Pippin poked her head out of the bedroom Dallas had turned into the tech room. "Good! You're here. Come on, Desi. Come on!"

Curious, but wary, she dropped her coat, hat and purse on the conference table and followed Ringo to the tech room. She debated telling Dallas about the oddball things happening her house. But Ringo would tease her mercilessly and she'd lose credibility as a debunker. In fact, quite a few Rampart members would take far too much satisfaction from her reports of paranormal activity.

Seeing Buck she stopped short. Damn, he was good-looking. His dark brown hair was cut short, almost military, and it gleamed with rich highlights. It took some effort to keep her eyes on his face rather than perusing his body and pondering how he'd look naked.

Dallas grabbed her arm and sat her on the chair facing a pair of computer monitors set up side by side. Desi held up her hands. "Tell me what's going on. You're all acting like nuts."

Pippin said, "Buck did a reading on Joan. The single mom with the crazy cousin."

"Uh-uh," Dallas interrupted. "No preliminaries. Let Desi see for herself."

Desi could have groaned. It was below zero outside, the weatherman predicted snowstorms, things were going wonky in her house, and Dallas dragged her across town for a psychic reading? Unless Buck had levitated or a camera had caught a full-body apparition who actually talked, Desi could not imagine what had them so excited.

"I will tell you this much," Dallas said. "Joan signed an affidavit. She and Buck never met before the reading." He pointed at himself then at Ringo and Pippin. "None of us told Buck any personal info. He didn't look at any of the video or recordings from our investigation at Joan's house."

"Okay."

"We covered the session with cameras, recorders and meters. We held it here to keep outside influence to a minimum." Dallas winked and patted a device sitting on the table. Desi didn't recognize what it was. "My new baby. It's a thermal camera."

"Wow," Desi said. She'd seen what other investigators captured on thermal cameras. Cold spots were a common phenomenon associated with paranormal activity. Since investigators and researchers had begun using thermal cameras, which recorded heat as opposed to light, there was a lot of documentation of what appeared to be apparitions. "That must have cost a fortune."

"It did." Dallas glowered at Ringo. "And any knucklehead who messes with it will end up with broken fingers." He sat and pulled a keyboard onto his lap. "I'm going to show you the regular video first."

Desi folded her arms and settled comfortably on the chair. She glanced at Buck. She got a distinct impression that the excitement and attention made him uncomfortable.

The screen came alive with a black-and-white video. Joan was a chunky woman. Seated, her knees and elbows drawn tight, she twisted a strand of hair around her fingers and appeared to be chewing gum. Buck sat on a chair facing her. He sat straight, his shoulders square and with his hands on his knees. Off camera Dallas stated the time, date and the names of the participants before he told Buck to begin. Worry flashed across Buck's face. He looked as if he wanted directions. Finally, his shoulders rose with a heavy breath and he smiled at Joan.

"Hi," he said. "You have kids."

Joan nodded. Her fingers twisted in her hair. "Two boys."

"What did you think of the investigation?"

Joan's fingers stilled and her face lit up with a smile. "It was great! I didn't expect it to be so, you know, professional." She giggled. "I'm really glad they didn't find ghosts. So what do we do now? I've never been to a psychic before."

Buck shifted on the chair and looked off-camera. "Um." He turned his attention back to Joan. "Is there anyone here who'd like to talk to Joan? My name is Buck Walker. If you want to show yourself I can see you."

Wait for it, Desi thought. She tapped her fingers against her upper arms.

On screen Buck raised his gaze and focused on a spot to the right of Joan. He smiled. "Hello," he said. Joan whipped her head about so fast she almost fell off the chair. Buck asked, "Can you talk? I can hear you if you do."

"Who's here?" Joan whispered. Her eyes were huge and round.

"A lady." He cocked his head, eyes narrowed. "I don't think she can talk."

Oh, boy, Desi thought. *Here it comes.*

Buck said, "She's showing me… Breast cancer?"

Joan gasped and clapped her hands over her mouth. The camera picked up the glitter of tears. Pippin appeared briefly to hand Joan a box of tissues. Buck wasn't looking at Joan at all, wasn't reading her body language or looking to her for clues. Niggling doubts tickled Desi.

"That's Olivia," Joan said. She kept looking around, trying to see what Buck saw. "My mother-in-law. My ex's mom. She stood by me and the boys when my ex took off. She got really sick and

I moved in to take care of her. I miss her so much. She's really here?"

Buck nodded. He was leaning back on the chair now, his shoulders relaxed and his smile easy. "Olivia, does Joan have to worry about any negative spirits in her house?" He jumped and laughed. "I will take that as a definite no." He said to Joan, "I don't think she likes your cousin scaring you."

"How is she?" Joan asked. "Is she okay? Can you tell her the boys talk about her all the time?" Her voice was croaky and she was working on her fifth or sixth tissue.

"She's good. Looks like a lovely lady. She's watching out for you and the boys. Olivia, is there anything you want to tell Joan?" He leaned forward, eyes narrowed in concentration. He shook his head. "I'm sorry, Olivia, I don't get it. Is that a will? Oh! Okay. It's life insurance."

Joan noisily blew her nose. "No. I cleaned out her house. There isn't any life insurance."

"She's saying there is." He nodded. "She's showing me an image of a man. Longish hair, skinny. Looks like he has a drug problem."

Joan's mouth fell open. "That's Robert! My ex-husband. That crackhead got life insurance from his mom?" She clenched her fists. "He hasn't paid a penny in child support. When the state goes after him he just quits whatever stupid job he has so they can't garnish his wages. Damn it, Olivia, why didn't you tell me he has money?"

Buck winced. "She's really sorry."

"So what do I do?"

Off-screen Pippin spoke. "There are some attorneys in town who do pro bono work for clients at the woman's shelter. I'll find one who'll go after Robert. It won't cost you anything."

Buck said, "She's showing me a calendar. What happens on March third?"

Joan began to cry again. She clutched the tissue box the way a troubled child held a toy. "My younger son's birthday."

Buck absently reached his left arm across his chest and patted his right shoulder. "She'll be at the party." Joan lost it completely. She bent over, sobbing wildly. Buck rubbed his face and looked as if he wanted to bolt. Then the video ended.

"Well?" Dallas asked. "What do you think, Desi?"

She blinked rapidly. A knot in her belly tightened her insides. She had to swallow several times before she felt she could speak in a normal tone. "That's interesting. Not at all what I expected." She turned to Buck. She didn't need psychic power to see his nervousness. It seemed a little strange to her that he cared what she thought. "No offense, Buck, but I have to play devil's advocate here."

"None taken," he said.

She ticked a finger. "First, every single thing you said is a public record. Names, birth and death certificates, addresses. The life insurance could be a lucky guess. That a mother would name her son beneficiary is a no-brainer. Ditto for deadbeat fathers."

Dallas made a disgusted noise, but Buck said, "Fair enough."

Dallas kicked her chair. "Hold on, Ms. Skeptic. You better see what we caught on the thermal."

Chapter Five

Desi watched with interest while Dallas cued the videos so the black-and-white video of the psychic reading showed on one screen and the thermal image showed on the other. Prickling with curious excitement, Desi suspected that Ringo had told the truth when he said this would rock her world. Little did he know it wouldn't take much to do that right now.

"There's no volume on the thermal, so I'm syncing it with the DVR. Ready?" Dallas tapped the keyboard.

The thermal image was bright with colors depicting temperatures on a scale. Buck and Joan were yellow outlines that turned orange then red at their cores. Behind them the air was blue and green. It looked like other thermal images Desi had seen. After Buck asked, "Is there anyone here who'd like to talk to Joan? My name is Buck Walker. If you want to show yourself I can see you," a dark spot formed slowly next to Joan.

Desi looked at the regular video. Nothing on that screen had changed.

The thermal image changed rapidly. The yellow outline around Buck turned hot pink and began to pulsate. A thick finger of pure white light swelled, reaching toward Joan. The images strobed with pink, purple and fluorescent orange lights. It looked like a 1960s psychedelic music video. Then Buck's voice said, "Hello. Can you talk? I can hear you if you do." The colors settled. On Joan's left side stood a dark red figure surrounded by white light.

Desi stared open-mouthed. She reminded herself to breathe.

While Buck and Joan talked, the apparition took on a feminine shape. Its heat signature was steady—unlike Buck's and Joan's, which shifted and had patches of blue and purple where their clothing blocked heat. When Buck asked about negative spirits the apparition flared white, and Buck reacted. As they talked about the life insurance the apparition began to grow pale and the white outline thinned. It soon lost its human shape, turning bloblike. It floated toward Buck. A finger of pale orange light stretched from the apparition and suddenly brightened. When Joan said, "My younger son's birthday," the distinct shape of a hand patted Buck on the shoulder. His hand moved to his shoulder and appeared to pat the ghostly hand. The apparition shrank and lost heat until it disappeared.

Dallas typed a few commands and the video images disappeared from the screens.

"Before you say anything, Desi," Dallas said, "I've been on the phone all day long with the thermal camera manufacturer. They've got no explanation for the freaky light show. We shot a couple hours of footage, trying to re-create what happened. We couldn't get it to do that again."

Desi felt like somebody had dumped a bucket of Ping-Pong balls inside her skull. She kept forgetting to breathe. Dallas and Ringo loved practical jokes, but when it came to paranormal research they didn't kid around. Even so, she suddenly understood how people with paranoid delusions felt. The crushing sense that everybody knew what she didn't, couldn't know. The sickening, humiliating fear that everyone was laughing at her, or plotting her destruction. Her scalp tightened until her face ached.

Buck touched her hand. She jumped to her feet, knocking her chair backward.

"I—I need some air," she stuttered, and rushed from the room. She stumbled to the front door, jerked it open and rushed outside into the cold night.

DESI STOOD beneath the lowered sky, the blanket of clouds turned yellow by city lights. She lifted her face and closed her eyes as fitful snowflakes touched her skin. Cold seeped through her jeans, stinging her thighs. Her head finally stopped spinning.

Crazy connections turned her brain into a funhouse where nothing was what it seemed. A coffee can spilling by itself—a man telling a woman he'd never met before that her mother-in-law's ghost was standing in the room. Her television turning on by itself—a red shape no human eye could see. Papers all over the floor, a blown cell phone… Did that twerp at the phone store actually accuse her of dropping it in water?

The storm door squeaked and Buck stepped onto the porch. "Are you all right?" He looked behind him, and closed the door. "If it's any consolation, that freaks me out, too."

As little as a week ago she'd have yelled at him and Dallas about concocting an elaborate hoax. She blinked away a snowflake that settled on her eyelashes. The cold had reached below her skin and she shivered. "You," she said with a snarl. "How did you know where I live?"

He eyed her warily.

"My neighbor saw you. I know you were there. How do you know when to call me? How do you even know it's me on the phone? How did you know where I shop? Or that I'd be at the antique store or that my sister was at Chico's? How come every time I talk to you or see you or even think about you my house goes crazy? You blew up my damned cell phone! How did you *do* that?"

He stepped off the porch, pulling off his coat, and draped it around her shoulders. The leather bomber jacket carried his heat and felt too good to refuse. The snow was coming down heavier, though it was far too cold for it to be wet. It pattered against her hair. She ducked her head and the scent of masculine leather and spice rose from the coat.

He rubbed the back of his head. Icy snowflakes glittered like diamonds on his dark hair. "I'm not doing anything."

"Then what the hell is going on? I've had to change more lightbulbs in the past few weeks than in the entire time I've lived in my house. I take a shower and I swear to God I hear somebody muttering at me. I go down in the basement and the door slams behind me. Something wiped everything off my desk. I had paper everywhere!" Her voice was getting squeaky and it horrified her, but she couldn't stop. "I'm getting scared of my own house. I am not scared of anything, but now I'm sleeping with the light on." She jammed a finger against his chest. It was like poking a piece of wood. "It's you! You're doing it. How am I supposed to deal with this?"

She started to poke him again, but he caught her hand.

"Tell me this is a joke," she said. "Tell me when I walk inside everybody will laugh. Ha ha, got one over on Desi. Tell me!"

He clasped her hand against his chest. His sweatshirt was cold, but she felt the heat of his skin beneath it. She blinked rapidly until she grasped a sliver of reason and could calm down a little. He stared into her eyes and saw black, liquid, soothing pools. He placed his other hand over hers, enveloping it with warmth. His gaze remained steady, hypnotic, until finally calm flowed through her body, erasing the chill in her bones and relaxing her muscles.

She dragged in a deep breath, then another. She could feel her pulse in her ears.

"It's not a joke," he said.

Hope withered, disappearing like a snowflake against warm skin. This was real. How it was real, how it could possibly, under any circumstances, be real, she did not know. But it was. She pulled her hand away from Buck's. As soon as the contact broke she missed his touch.

The front door opened and Pippin peered out. "Hey, guys, is everything okay?"

Desi's world hadn't merely rocked. It had turned upside down and inside out. She felt like one of those goofy kids she'd known in college who were always slouching around asking Big Questions: What is the meaning of life? Do we really exist? How do we know anything?

How did *she* know anything?

She shrugged off Buck's coat and handed it back to him.

"Come inside, Desi," Pippin said. "It's freezing out here."

Embarrassment over what she'd said to Buck replaced the fear. There had to be a reasonable, logical, scientific explanation for what was happening in her house, as well as what she'd seen on the thermal camera video. She had to figure it out. She had to or else concede that Sasquatch, the Loch Ness monster and UFOs might be real, too.

She and Buck returned to the apartment, where Dallas and Ringo now sat at the conference table eating chips with dip. Both men eyed her with apprehension. She plastered a big smile on her face. "It's official, guys. I have been spooked."

Pippin gave her a one-armed hug that only served to deepen Desi's embarrassment. She shoved her anxiety into a mental closet and slammed the door.

Dallas zeroed in on Desi. "How do we go about debunking this?"

She looked at Buck. If he'd looked the least bit smug, or showed a trace of calculating gleam as he mulled over how he could make money off his talent, she would walk out for good. He wore a sheepish smile and appeared to find a spot on the table worthy of study.

"You got me. I don't have a clue how to explain it."

"Want to watch it again?"

Anxiety scratched at the mental door. "Maybe later. What are you going to do with it, Dallas?" She eased onto a chair. Buck was watching her and she didn't need to be a psychic to know it.

Dallas played a tattoo on the table. He ate a few chips, crunching loudly. "The reading didn't take place in a controlled environment. We tried, but there were too many outside influences like the sun and electricity and the fact that I just got the thermal camera and I'm not experienced with all its quirks."

Ringo added, "Like you said, Desi, there's no way to prove Joan's not a ringer or Buck didn't do a background check beforehand."

"And," added Buck, "As you said, life insurance could be a lucky guess."

Desi looked at him. When he smiled she felt the same soothing warmth she'd felt when he held her hand.

"We've got plenty of time to go over it," Dallas said. "This is one piece of evidence we can never post on the Web site, even in the members-only section, and we can't share it with other groups. This can't get out."

"Why?" Desi asked.

"It's me," Buck said, with an apologetic note.

Ringo said, "Even if we blur his features and don't use his name, somebody will figure it out. His identity will be all over the Internet." Ringo loosed a hearty laugh. "He'll have to go into the Witness Protection Program to get away from all his fans."

Desi believed it. Her sister, Gwen, would be first in line.

"A bigger problem is my job," Buck said. "If defense attorneys find out CSPD has a psychic on the force they'll reopen every case where I've testified in court."

Every so-called psychic Desi had run across was an attention junkie. She couldn't turn on the television without finding a program about the paranormal. Psychics vied for the chance to appear on talk shows and documentaries. Some psychics had their own TV or radio shows. What if people with genuine abilities were like Buck? Everyday people trying to live normal lives. People who didn't want fame, fortune or a cadre of groupies.

Dallas said, "I'm taking the camera to an expert to be checked out. I might take it to two. Plus I'm taking the videos to Professor Moreno over at the university. He can help us figure out a way to run controlled experiments."

"We need to be cautious," Pippin said. "I'm on the fence about demonic activity, but I don't think it's something we should mess with. We have to make sure we aren't summoning evil. Right, Buck? You mentioned negative entities. What did you call them?"

"Dark Presences. I think they're the Shadow People other people see." He shifted uncomfortably. "Or maybe they are demons. I don't know. They're different."

If his shaky voice was any indication, Desi figured those Dark Presences scared the hell out of him. She felt a clutch of fear. No way could a Dark Presence follow her home, no matter what kind of stupid invitation she offered. She wondered about the little boy they'd "talked" to in the Moore house, wondered if her house was his new playground. After what she'd seen this evening, anything seemed possible.

SHOULDERS BACK, determined, Desi walked into her house. As she'd been leaving Rampart headquarters Buck had invited her to Starbucks for coffee. She didn't need psychic ability to know he wanted to talk about the activity in her house. She'd declined. She could handle this problem on her own.

She hung up her coat and put down her purse. Spike greeted her and she patted his back. "Any ghosties, big boy?" He wandered into the kitchen, grumbling about the state of his food dish. She fed him.

In the middle of the living room Desi put her hands on her hips. "Okay," she said. "Your name is Jonathon, right? All right, honey, we need to talk. This is my house. I bought it with my money. Every single thing in this house is mine and I don't appreciate you messing with my stuff."

Even alone, with nobody around to hear, except the cat, she felt like an idiot.

"I'm really sorry you died and got stuck in that old house with nobody to play with. I didn't mean to ask you to come to my place. It was a mistake. If you want to find your family and friends, you have to leave. Go toward the light. Everybody you ever knew is over there. I bet you were a nice kid, but I don't want you here. I don't want a roommate. You are trespassing. So get out of here. No hard feelings, but you have to go away."

She waited for lightbulbs to blow or the television to turn on or for the sound of footsteps on the second floor.

"It's better this way, honey. Trust me. You'll be happy when you find your family. So you be a good boy and get out of my house."

DESI HIT the Print command, and the laser printer fired up to spit out pages of reports. It was tax season. While businesses had accountants to handle tax returns, Desi had to make sure every receipt and invoice was accounted for and every penny balanced so they could do their jobs. She kept up throughout the year, but inevitably business owners began to panic beginning in January.

She pulled the stack of reports off the printer tray, checked to make sure every page had printed correctly, stapled the pages and slipped it all into the proper folder. She made a face at the rolling file cart, crammed full of hanging folders. Her spare bedroom was lined with more filing cabinets bursting with paperwork that needed to be retained for seven years in case the IRS came snooping around her clients. If she picked up even one more client she'd have to rent a storage unit.

Or concede it was time to rent office space in a commercial building. Until now she resisted the idea. She liked working out of her home, and she really liked being able to work in her pajamas.

She opened the next client's file.

"Veronica!"

Desi screamed. She pushed with her heels, sending the chair skittering backward, and it clunked against the coffee table. She jumped to her feet, fists clenched, ready to fight.

Heart in her throat, she looked around. The house had an open floor plan with the kitchen and living room separated by a breakfast counter. From where she stood she could see the front door past the kitchen and the sliding glass doors leading to the small balcony in back.

A movement startled her.

Spike, wild-eyed, his ears laid into sharp, devilish points, crouched on the top step of the stairs. Every hair on his body stood on end. His poofy tail slashed the air. She could hear him growling.

The growl undid her. Her nearly falling off the chair would have scared him, but only dogs could make him growl like a leopard.

A dog hadn't yelled in her ear.

She snatched a stapler off her desk. Holding it raised, ready to smash an intruder's face, she crept toward the kitchen, the only possible place someone could hide.

No one crouched in the kitchen. Desi exchanged the stapler for a heavy-duty flashlight and searched the town house top to bottom, investigating even the skimpiest nooks and crannies. Spike accompanied her. His fur settled and his tail returned to a skinny whip, but he remained skittish.

Desi kept waiting for her mind to come up with

a rational explanation. She'd dozed off and dreamed the yell. A neighbor had turned up the television volume. A power surge had pulsed through the radio and blared a random signal. The salad she'd eaten for dinner contained magic mushrooms and she was hallucinating.

No, that shout in her ear had been real. She'd *felt* it.

It hadn't been a little kid, either. That had been a man's voice, deep and angry.

"Okay, buster, let's get this straight. This is my house! I don't tolerate living people yelling at me and I'm sure not taking it from you." She glanced right, left, up and down. "I mean it. You don't belong here so get out right now."

She waited. And waited. Her back and shoulders began to ache with tension. How in the world did somebody actually know when a ghost had left? Only one person could tell her.

She snatched up her cell phone and scrolled through the log of incoming calls until she found Buck's number. Her thumb hovered over the Send button.

This new phone worked perfectly, with even better reception than the old phone. It still ticked her off that the pimply-faced clerk at the phone store insisted she had to have dropped the phone in water in order to fry the circuits. Like she'd lie just to get a twenty-dollar trade-in on the ruined phone. The new one still cost a hundred and fifty dollars, and that was after the mail-in rebate.

Feeling foolish, and glad it was after midnight so

none of her neighbors could see her outside in pajamas freezing her butt off, she called Buck.

SO MUCH FOR NOT looking like an idiot. When Buck answered the phone his voice was husky with sleep. Desi apologized for calling in the middle of the night, but he had laughed and said, "It's okay. I don't have to be to work until five-thirty."

When he arrived at her house, she said, "You didn't have to come."

Those broad shoulders of his lifted in a shrug. "I was awake anyway. So tell me what's going on."

Desi couldn't launch into the explanation in the hallway. She offered him a drink and invited him to sit in the living room. Playing hostess delayed the inevitable.

When Spike hopped onto the love seat next to Buck, she warned him, "Watch out! He's mean."

Tail high and welcoming, Spike stepped onto Buck's lap and butted his head against the man's chin. Buck honed in on Spike's happy spot, scratching him lightly behind the ears. Desi had never seen the cat glom onto a stranger like this. When Desi reached for the cat, he hunkered down and gave her a warning glare. *Try it,* he seemed to say.

"It's okay," Buck said. "I like cats." He stroked a big hand over yellow-orange fur. "You haven't returned my calls."

In the days since she'd seen the thermal video Buck had left two voice mails. His concern touched her, but it also increased her embarrassment over how she'd acted. She'd been seriously considering quitting Rampart. She'd had enough woo-woo stuff to last the rest of her life and if she never even heard the word *paranormal* again, that would be perfectly fine.

"I needed some time to think."

"About?"

You. She liked Buck Walker. She liked his calmness, his voice and the way he looked. But his…gift! No matter how times she replayed the session videos in her mind, she couldn't come up with a single rationalization for what she'd seen. The only answer seemed to be that Buck was the real thing, and that meant everything she believed disappeared into smoke. It meant her goofy sister had been right all along when it came to ghosts.

Still, she liked him.

"Just stuff," she finally said. "I'm thinking about quitting Rampart. If ghosts are real, then what's the point of being a skeptic? It just makes me look stubborn."

He nodded as if that made perfect sense.

"But that's not why I called you." She fiddled with a loose thread on her ratty sweater, wishing she'd put on something nicer. She hadn't even brushed her hair. She pointed at her desk where the screensaver scrolled the message "I ain't 'fraid of no ghost," across the monitor. "I was working. The house was quiet—no TV or radio. Spike was sleeping in his basket. A man yelled in my ear." She closed her eyes. "Right in my ear, like he had leaned over my shoulder. I felt his breath! I almost fell off the chair."

"What did he say?"

"One word. 'Veronica.'"

Buck's eyes widened.

"That means something?" she asked him. "I don't know anybody named Veronica."

"Didn't you read the research on the Moore house that Tara posted on the Web site?"

"Sure. The little boy who died. Jonathon. I told him to go away. It's been quiet. Nothing has happened. Until tonight, that is."

"You need to look at what else Tara found. Veronica Skillihorn was murdered in that house. Up on the third floor where I saw the Dark Presence. That's what you invited home."

Chapter Six

Buck rubbed his eyes. He was wide awake, but his eyes ached with fatigue. Desi gave him a tour of her house. In cop mode, he checked doors and windows for security, and for anything that struck him as out of place. He went through the unfinished basement, the main floor and the two bedrooms and bathroom on the second floor. He found nothing.

He did notice that top to bottom her house was squeaky clean and uncluttered. It might have been cold, even sterile, if not for the warm colors.

Desi didn't possess much in way of belongings, but everything was quality. Like his mother used to say, "Not much, but picked with care."

Only her bed gave him pause. Desi was small enough to sleep comfortably on the love seat in the living room but she had a king-size bed. It seemed out of sync with her minimalist style—unless she had an active, athletic sex life. He doubted it. When he'd run into Gwen at Chico's, Gwen had assured him that Desi was free and single, and *knowing* told him Desi didn't pick up men in bars. Still, he couldn't help imagining Desi draped in filmy chiffon, stretched out on the bed, smiling seductively. It distracted him from searching with his inner eye for signs of the Dark Presence.

When he returned to the living room, Desi asked, "Well? See anything?"

He kept getting impressions of the motherly figure he'd seen around Desi before. Her presence relieved him. Benign, friendly spirits usually fled the area when a Dark Presence showed up.

"It's quiet," he said. He glimpsed a sparkle near the love seat. He felt the ghostly presence like cool, soft cloth draped across his skin. "I could use a glass of water. Do you mind?"

When she went into the kitchen he faced the love seat and whispered, "I can see you."

The spirit's delight passed through his body. A disconcerting sensation, though pleasant. Her image took shape enough for him to see an older woman with light hair. The sparkles he'd been seeing turned out to be gaudy jewelry. Her facial features were vague, but he saw her smile.

Desi returned and handed him a glass of water.

"I guess that shows you have to be talking to the right ghost," she said. "Before I told the little boy to go away. Tonight I told the big guy to get lost." She widened her eyes.

She wanted affirmation, but Buck pretended to not know that. It would take a lot more than being yelled at to make a Dark Presence go away. Besides, he liked Desi the way she was now. No-nonsense, feisty, acting as if when she got her hands on a ghost it would be sorry.

Don't think about the bed, he told himself. Quit thinking about her pretty eyes and wondering if her creamy skin was as soft as it looked.

"Maybe it's a poltergeist." Even as she spoke she shook her head. "It looks like poltergeist activity. Except, conditions are not right for poltergeists."

"How so?" He sensed the female spirit's interest in the conversation. She lingered close to Desi, but the only thing visible was her jewelry. Buck could just make out a large brooch and part of a necklace. He downed the water and handed the glass to Desi. "Could I get a refill?" As soon as she returned to the kitchen, he whispered, "I don't think she's ready to talk to you right now. Sorry." He picked up Spike. The big cat curled contentedly over his arm. His purr rumbled.

When she returned, Desi said, "Every single case of poltergeist activity Rampart has investigated has had one common denominator. Teenage girls. We have tons of anecdotes, but we've never documented anything. One theory is that poltergeist activity comes from the girls. They're doing it on purpose, or unconsciously, or maybe raging hormones create physical manifestation. Speaking from my own experience as a former teenage girl, most of them go through a phase where the occult is fascinating and they're hyper-suggestible." She handed him the fresh water.

"Were you?"

"Me?" Her cheeks pinked. "Not like my sister and her friends. They held midnight séances and played with mirrors and Ouija boards. In any case, my neighbor on one side is an older widow and on the other side is a thirty-something couple with no kids. No teenagers."

Buck said, "What I saw was no poltergeist."

"Why are you afraid of them? The Dark Presences? Do you think they're demons?"

He drained the water glass. When he handed the glass back to Desi, Spike struggled to reach it. He set the cat on the floor.

"Maybe," Buck said. "I've seen five or six of them. It's not good to let them know I can see them." He refrained from watching the female spirit moving around the room. She wanted his attention. Her cool energy turned cold and Desi shivered. Intuition said that now was not the time. Desi had been badly shaken by the disembodied voice. Now she was calm and he preferred she stayed that way.

"I'm not totally close-minded. I've seen enough to realize the chances are good there's another plane of existence. A paranormal plane that occasionally seeps over into our perception of the world. What I don't believe is that dead people hang around to harass the living."

He got the distinct impression of the female spirit

shrugging and showing her palms in the universal gesture meaning, *What are you going to do?* He caught his lower lip in his teeth to keep from laughing.

Desi moved restlessly to the breakfast bar and stopped, facing the front door.

Petite and compact though she might be, her rear end was round and lush, beckoning exploring hands. From upstairs the king-sized bed seemed to call his name.

"Desi?"

She turned around. "I'm so embarrassed right now. I dragged you here on a wild goose chase. It's stupid to get scared."

"Every time I put on the uniform I get scared," Buck said. "It keeps me alive. Not a bad thing."

"Oh, please. You don't get scared."

Spoken as if she knew him. "You want fear? Try a traffic stop. You can't see a guy's hands, don't know what the passengers are going to do. Could be a drunk, or a crazy, or some guy drunk and crazy. Smart cops stay scared."

"I hate being scared. It makes my stomach hurt."

"Maybe it's time to contact Alec Viho," Buck said.

She laughed, but it had an edge. "I don't need him stinking up my house with burning sage."

He glanced at his wristwatch. When he saw the late hour, as if reminded, fatigue weighted his eyelids. Five-thirty was going to come fast. *If* he ever got Desi and that oversize playground of a bed out of his head so he could sleep. "At least think about it. Alec has a lot of power. It's all around him."

"Right." She paced, clutching her elbows with twitchy fingers.

"Just think about it," he repeated. The presence of her guardian spirit reassured him. As long as she was around, Desi was safe. "If you're still nervous, go to your sister's."

Or my place.

"I'm fine."

"Okay." He picked up his coat. "But I need some sleep."

She looked away and he placed a hand against her arm. When she didn't move away, he rubbed her upper arm. The well-worn fibers of her sweater were soft and nubby, hinting at the warmth of her skin. He wondered what would happen if he suggested he stay the rest of the night. "You can call me anytime. Night or day."

She lifted her head. Her sideways gaze, her blue eyes shadowed by luxurious lashes, turned him to mush. Except in his groin, which wasn't feeling at all mushy. If she suggested chaining him at her front door like a watchdog, he'd do it.

"Are you hitting on me?" Her voice held a smoky note.

"Do you want me to?"

She dropped her gaze. "No."

No surprise, but it was disappointing. Bench-pressing a hundred and fifty pounds took less effort than it took to pull his hand away. "Too bad. The offer stands anyway. Call me night or day. I live to protect and serve."

He left her then. Fat snowflakes settled on his hair and stung his face. He welcomed the cold, hoping it would cool his heated blood. He got into the Jeep and fired the engine. God, she was beautiful. And sexy. He didn't need psychic ability to realize she had the power to drive him out of his mind.

He reached out to grab the gearshift and a woman appeared in the passenger seat.

His foot slipped off the clutch. The Jeep lurched and died. "Shit! Don't do that!"

The spirit gazed at him. He saw her clearly by the dashboard lights. Her hair was smooth and shoulder-length. She had elegant features that reminded him of Gwen. When she smiled he saw traces of Desi, too. Their mother, he guessed. He waited a second for his heart to slow.

"I'll tell her about you. Eventually. When she's in the mood. Why are you visiting me?"

Her smile faded and so did some of her glow.

"Not a talker, huh?" He restarted the Jeep. "Did Desi let the Dark Presence in?" The spirit actually shuddered. He took that as a yes. "Do you know where it is right now?" She shook her head. "Can you let me know if it comes back? If it bothers her?" The spirit canted her head as if the idea had never occurred to her. Her hair shifted, revealing an oversize earring with glittering stones. She nodded. "Is there anything I can do for Desi right now? Help her feel better?" She lifted her fingers to her pursed lips and blew him a kiss.

"DID I REALLY SAY THAT?" Desi asked the cat. Spike prowled the room, his tail an agitated semaphore signaling his desire to knock something onto the floor. "'Are you hitting on me?' Really? That's something Gwen would say."

Gwen would definitely say something like that to Buck Walker. Given half a chance, Gwen would snatch him up, twist him around in a passion tornado then drop him, dazed and never knowing what hit him.

It annoyed her that she'd said no to him. Not that she knew him well enough to jump into bed with him, but it couldn't hurt to see if he was a good kisser. She licked her lips, unsure exactly how long it had been since anyone had kissed her. His name had been Ted, or Ned. His kisses hadn't left much of an impression. Everything Buck did left an impression.

He'd have stayed if she'd asked.

Idiot.

To distract herself Desi turned on the television. She flipped through the channels until she found an infomercial where excited people swooned over the unlimited possibilities of a pasta cooker. She turned the volume down low as a buffer against silence and went to the kitchen to make a cup of tea. Later, cradling the hot cup in both hands, waiting for the warmth to seep into her cold palms, she studied her desk. She wondered how much time it would take to move everything around so she could work with her back to the wall.

Anger tightened her scalp.

She drew a deep, steadying breath and marched to the desk. She set down the teacup and plopped onto the chair. She opened the file for an Old Colorado City boutique. She stared at the screen and her eyes burned. Fatigue weighted her shoulders as if a heavy blanket had dropped over them.

She closed the file and the program, turned off the printer and moved the cursor over the Internet icon. She'd check her mail then go to bed.

Compulsion gripped her. She needed things to make sense. She brought up the Rocky Mountain Paranormal Research Team Web site.

The Web site was deceptively simple looking. Dallas liked to say, "Any goober can build a Web site, but most shouldn't. There's art involved." All the sites he built and maintained for clients were clean, informative and easy to navigate. The Rampart site received thousands of hits every day, and the forums were always full of comments, criticisms, arguments and pleas for help with pesky spirits.

Desi signed in with her user name and password,

which took her to the members-only page. She found the research Tara had done on the Moore house. She skimmed through the info she'd already read and found the newest postings.

The house had been built in 1888 by Charles Josiah Skillihorn, a silver miner. He'd been a friend of Gen. William Jackson Palmer, the railroad baron who had founded the city of Colorado Springs. Palmer had earned a memorial statue that towered over the intersection of Platte and Nevada in the center of downtown, but Skillihorn was mostly forgotten. In 1892 twenty-one-year-old Veronica Eugenia Skillihorn née Shriver, had traveled from Boston to Colorado to marry Skillihorn. Tara had put in a note: "Mail-order bride?"

Seeing Veronica's name sent a frisson of ice along Desi's spine. Her neck itched with the urge to look over her shoulder.

Information on the Skillihorns was sketchy until 1898, when Veronica was murdered. Newspaper reports of the crime were florid and sensational. Writers referred to Veronica as a "beautiful and tragic angel on Earth" and Charles as "stoic, taciturn and brave, maintaining a stony facade against grief as great as the majestic Pikes Peak." The murderer was referred to as that "hulking, beastly Italian gardener."

"How politically incorrect," Desi muttered, and waded through the stories where it seemed the reporters collected bonuses for every adjective and adverb.

Skillihorn had returned to his home after a two-week absence. He discovered his wife's body in the bedroom on the third floor. She'd been beheaded with a scythe.

"Eww." Desi scrolled down the page.

The scythe belonged to the gardener, an immigrant named Arturio Carpetti, who worked as a gardener for the Skillihorns. According to the newspaper, Skillihorn had discovered "the murderous brute, soaked to the skin with the precious life fluids of his tragic victim," hiding in the garden shed. "It is testimony to a great man's noble nature that he refrained from dispatching the Italian monster with the very scythe that had robbed this world of a beautiful Angel." Apparently Skillihorn had "thrashed" the evil murderer to within an inch of his life. No one would have blamed him if he'd killed the man.

There were several newspaper illustrations of Carpetti's trial. In every drawing he was depicted as a hunched and hulking brute with beetled brows and a snaggletoothed snarl. The judge and jury were men in starched collars, with perfect posture and solemn expressions. One illustration showed Charles Skillihorn seated in the gallery. The artist had captured the grieving husband in profile and made him look like a tragic Greek god. The trial had taken one day. Carpetti was hanged two weeks later. Over one thousand people had attended the execution to "assure their wounded and fearful minds that the Italian monster was properly dispatched to Hell to meet His Divine Justice."

Desi scrolled further down and groaned. "Oh, Tara! You didn't!"

Tara Chase had posted crime scene photographs. Even in grainy, poorly lit black-and-white they were gruesome. Desi recognized an elaborately carved window casing from the Moore house. Veronica's headless, blood-soaked corpse looked like something from a slasher movie. Another photograph showed her head. Desi thanked God that tangles of matted hair covered Veronica's face. Seeing the victim's wide terrified eyes and soundless scream would have insured Desi never got to sleep this night.

Desi logged off.

Seeing Spike calmly asleep in his basket soothed her tattered nerves. Desi got sick and tired of people claiming their pets saw ghosts. *It's true! Fluffy stares at the corner. I know she's seeing something!* At this moment, though, Desi was willing to accept that Spike's stillness meant she was alone.

DESI ENTERED the warmth and noise of Chico's restaurant. The smell of green chilies and roasting pork made her mouth water. In the hub of downtown the restaurant had been a fixture for over thirty years. It was always crowded with students from the university, tourists and regulars who knew where to find the best margaritas.

When Gwen called to say she and the girls were at Chico's and Desi should join them, Desi jumped on it.

She spotted Gwen waving at her from a table near the door leading to the patio and next to the tiny dance floor and stage. It was the only table in the place away from the main dining area. Amber and Pam, Gwen's friends, laughed it up with two men. One of the men was Buck Walker.

A setup.

What the hell. With a choice between suffering her sister's matchmaking or returning home where every little noise made her jump, she chose her sister. Besides, at Chico's she got guacamole.

Buck stood as she approached and pulled out the chair next to his. How convenient that Gwen and the girls surrounded the other man at the opposite end of the table, leaving plenty of room for Desi to get cozy with Buck.

Gwen did that hand-waving so-happy-to-see-you thing she did. "Hi, sweetie! Sit down! More margaritas are on the way." She draped an arm over the man's shoulders. "Will, this is my big sister, Desi. Desi, Will."

Eyes overly bright and smiling crookedly, Will slurred, "Pleased to meetcha, big sister."

"Hi." She peeled out of her coat and Buck hung it on a wall hook. She settled on the wooden chair and asked, "Did you know she called me?"

"Maybe. What would you like to drink?"

"Come to the dark side," Gwen said. "Where the Mighty Margarita River flows."

Gwen lived three blocks away. She could crawl home if she had to. Desi had to drive. "Hot coffee."

Buck signaled a server. "Hungry?" When she said she'd like chips and guacamole, Buck ordered for her. He asked for another Coke.

"No Margarita River for you?" Desi asked him.

Buck shook his head. "I have to work tomorrow." He grinned at his friend, who sprawled on his chair while three gorgeous blondes fed him from a plate of enchiladas. "I'm DD. Designated Driver."

Desi covered her mouth with a hand to keep from laughing at the goofiness going on at the other end of the table. Another pitcher of margaritas would make them obnoxious, but right now they were funny. The three women practically draped themselves over Will who had closely cropped brown hair and the clean-cut features of a 1960s teen idol. "Is your friend a policeman, too?"

"Yeah. We went through the academy together." He leaned his forearms on the table and held his head low. His sweater sleeves were pushed up, revealing muscular arms. She wondered if he worked out or if he'd been born gorgeous.

"How's it going with you?"

"Okay."

He gave her a sideways look. "Anything going on at your house?"

She aimed for a flip answer, to tell him that everything was absolutely fine and she must have imagined that harsh voice after all. His solemn demeanor and palpable concern quelled flippancy.

"I don't know."

"You don't know?"

"I don't know if I'm hearing things because I'm hearing things or because I'm scared I'm hearing things. I'm a little jumpy these days."

"I actually understand that."

The server set drinks and guacamole in front of her and Buck, and a fresh pitcher of margaritas at the other end of the table. Behind them, two men set up the tiny stage for a live performance. Fridays and Saturdays rocked at Chico's. When the music started it would be impossible to hear herself think, much less hold a conversation.

Buck scooped guacamole onto a handpressed and flash-fried tortilla chip. "May I?" he asked.

"Sure."

Instead of eating it, he guided it to her mouth. Surprised, she bit it. The pepper bite filled her mouth with fire. She chewed, swallowed then ate the rest from his hand.

"Whew! I should have ordered water. That's good!"

"Like it hot, eh?" He offered her a drink of his Coke.

Desi glimpsed her sister grinning at her. Gwen mugged, rolling her eyes and pursing her lips and pretending to swoon as if Desi were the only person who could see her. Desi turned on the chair, putting the Blonde-keteers and their happy victim out of her line of vision.

It was easy to shut out the noise and gaiety of Chico's on Friday night with Buck Walker to focus on. They shared the guacamole and small talk, his low voice for her ears only. She liked him, she decided. Maybe, just maybe, there was potential for him be more than a buddy.

When a musician began tuning his guitar and doing sound checks, Desi cringed anticipating the cacophony to come.

"I need to get home," she told Buck.

He glanced at his wristwatch. "I should go, too." He pounded the table with the flat of his hand. "Will! Hey! We need to blow out of here, man."

Will groaned loudly. "Oh, man! Wait awhile, Buck-a-roo. I promised these lovely ladies a dance." The three Blonde-keteers pouted prettily and begged Buck to let Will play a little bit longer. One dance, they promised. Just one.

"You've been outvoted," Desi whispered in his ear. He smelled of woodsy aftershave and pepper spice. She wondered what he'd do if she licked his ear. "Hand me my coat."

"Let me buy you an ice cream," he said. His breath caressed her cheek.

"Ice cream? It's twenty degrees out there!"

"Then it won't be crowded at Mitzi's."

"They aren't even open this late."

"Can't hurt to check. I'll get you hot fudge."

The guitarist hit a loud, drawn-out chord. Desi winced at the reverb. Better to discuss this outside than in here. "Let's go," she said.

He helped her into her coat. When he adjusted and smoothed the collar, his thumbs eased along her neck. Her hands tingled. She kissed and hugged Gwen, Amber and Pam. When Will stretched out his arms and pursed his lips for a kiss, she sidestepped and patted his head.

"It was very nice meeting you, Will."

He grinned up at her. "Ya know, for a big sister you sure are little."

"Good night," she said. Buck took her arm and guided her through the rowdy crowd, using his body to prevent any clumsy boots or careless elbows from finding her.

The cold night air actually felt good. She sucked in a big breath to cool her still stinging mouth. Other than people hurrying indoors or toward parked vehicles, Desi and Buck had the sidewalk to themselves.

A recent snowstorm had dumped nearly eight inches of snow on parts of the city. Today the temperature had risen to over forty degrees, so the gutters were filled with sloppy wet snow piles and ice.

At the far corner, she could see the darkened storefront of Mitzi's Ice Cream and Candy Shoppe, a Tejon Street fixture since the 1950s. "Told you," she said. "Closed."

"Worth a shot," he said. He touched the side of her hand with his, and when she didn't pull away, he enfolded her hand in his. He turned west, ambling, peering at storefronts and the turn-of-century brick buildings that housed them. "I like this town."

"Are you from Colorado?"

"Nebraska," he said. He stopped and studied a display of used books. "Town called Winnow Corners. Heard of it?"

She thought about it then shook her head. She liked holding his hand. "Can't say that I have."

"Huh. I'm surprised. It has almost four hundred people."

A gust of wind curled around the corner, flipping her hair and tearing the warmth from her cheeks. "The wind is too cold. And I really have to get home. I have to meet a client tomorrow morning."

"Can't get him to reschedule for midnight?" he teased and turned around. He turned loose her hand. Before she could register the loss, he draped an arm around her shoulders as if it were the most natural thing in the world. He snuggled her against his body.

The art gallery on the corner had a breezeway. An L-shaped, glass-sided display shielded it from the sidewalk. Inside the breezeway, windows held framed art, ceramics, bronze sculptures and exquisitely handcrafted jewelry. An elaborate neck collar in silver set with dark-blue stones caught her eye. It looked more appropriate for hanging on a wall than actually wearing, but it was beautiful.

"You don't wear jewelry," Buck said.

"Gwen wears enough for both of us. I like looking at it, though."

"Who else wears lots of jewelry?"

The question came from so far out of left field, she hadn't a clue how to answer. He looked beyond her. She followed his gaze and saw their reflection in the glass. A thump hit her belly, rocking her hips and weakening her knees. He was so tall that even in two-inch heels, the top of her head barely reached his shoulder.

He met her gaze in the glass. His smile turned her insides liquid. When he placed a hand along her cheek and turned her face up to his, she couldn't have protested even if she thought she should.

"You're beautiful," he whispered. He lowered his face slowly, always watching her eyes. When his mouth hovered less than an inch over hers, she closed the gap. His mouth was gentle and tasted spicy. Her chest grew too tight to breathe. When he slid the tip of his tongue slowly along her upper lip, she parted her lips, inviting him in.

He enfolded her, pressing her against his body, shielding her from the wind. He entwined his fingers in her hair and held the back of her head.

He was twice her size and knew the life-saving fighting skills of a street cop, but Desi felt her own power. She soared on it. She pressed her advantage, dueling with his tongue. When he made a tiny, choked noise in his throat, she knew she could take him to his knees.

She pulled slowly away from his kiss. He nibbled the corner of her mouth and pressed hot kisses on her cheek and the line of her jaw. Her knee and hip joints seemed to have wandered to a bench to watch the action. Desi wobbled, resting her weight for a second against his big hand at the small of her back.

"I really need to get home." She tensed, waiting, hoping, he'd offer to accompany her.

"I guess," he said, reluctantly. He eased strands of hair off her face.

He released her, and the corners of his mouth curled in a smile. "I'm hitting on you. Do you mind?"

"No."

His smile widened. Looking so pleased with himself that Desi almost laughed, he walked her to her car. After she slid behind the wheel, he leaned against the open door. "Are you doing anything Tuesday evening?"

"Tuesday?"

"Wednesdays and Thursdays are my days off. If you're free, how about dinner and a movie?"

She answered, "Sure, I'd love it" before reason huffed in annoyance. She'd never had a one-night stand but plenty of onetime dates. The men who seemed so interesting before she went out with them quickly revealed their flaws and foibles.

"You're too picky," Gwen always told her. "Give a guy a chance instead of going over him with a microscope. So what if his car is dirty or he leaves a chintzy tip or forgets to open a door?"

Realization hit her like a rock in the gut. It wasn't the men. They were human, after all, and nobody was perfect. *She* was the problem. Her high standards hadn't led her to Mr. Right. Her supercilious attitude meant any Mr. Right with half a brain would stay far, far away from her. A sick feeling warned her that she was going to blow it with Buck.

"Six?" he asked. "Early dinner, late movie?"

"Sounds great," she said. He closed the car door and stepped onto the sidewalk, watching her drive away.

She ran her tongue over her lips, still tasting him.

At home, Spike met her at the door. He twined around her legs and complained in squeaky meows. She scooped him up and hugged him tight. He grumbled and slashed his tail, but made no move to escape.

"I think we're two of a kind. Always acting grouchy and hard to get along with, but we love to be held. Don't we? We like Buck, too." She gave the cat a big kiss between the ears and set him on the floor.

"Now if I can figure out a way to not blow this."

Chapter Seven

Desi dreamed of Buck. He held her wrists, pressing them into the soft mattress, his body superheated along the length of hers. He kissed her senseless, hot, wet, commanding. *Touch me. Please touch me,* she pleaded, and he trailed his fingers along her arms, slow and teasing, melting her clothing as if parting mist instead of flannel. She struggled to bring her legs around his hips, but he pinned her flat, his hips undulating slowly, tormenting her with heat. He kissed her chin, her throat, the delicate lines of her collarbones. She tried to hold him, but her arms were useless, weighted, helpless. All she could do was moan as he closed his mouth over her breast. Touch me…touch me…touch me.

He stroked her body, and she could see the lines of heat in red and purple and gold making her skin glow as if on fire. He grasped her face in both hands and kissed her mouth, consuming her, melding their bodies. She couldn't breathe. He was so heavy, so hot. She tried to move, tried to tell him he smothered her, and she yearned to touch him, but she could not move. His hands caressed her neck. His thumbs pressed lightly into her flesh, then he squeezed, his fingers tightening. She gasped for air and her lungs began to scream.

Her eyes flew open. Blackness loomed over her face. Shadow within shadow, blacker than black. Stars danced before her vision and her eardrums pulsed. The fingers at her neck tightened. She tried to scream, tried to fight, but her body felt like lead.

Needles pierced her. An unearthly yowl shattered the paralysis like ice. She fought for her life, flailing and punching at air. She battled hot needles and the crushing weight on her chest. She twisted and screamed. She grabbed something large and muscular and tried to fling it away. For a moment it refused to budge. When she tore the weight away, she screamed again as skin went with it.

Gasping with the spasms in her throat, struggling to breathe, she groped for the light, knocked a book to the floor and finally found the switch.

Spike stood at the end of the bed. His eyes were black and his fur stood, making him look twice his size. With his ears laid flat his head was a ball of fury. Back arched, he hissed and growled.

She looked down at her chest where deep scratches leaked blood onto her pajama top.

"You son of a bitch!" She threw a pillow at the cat and he streaked out of the bedroom. She could hear him growling in the hallway.

She coughed as her throat spasmed again. Her chest was on fire. Damned cat must have been sleeping on her throat. She stumbled out of bed and tried to shake away the image of the black figure pinning her to the mattress, smothering her… strangling her.

On rubbery legs she made it to the bathroom and turned on the light. Blood splotched her pajama top and leaked from a bite on her chin. She fumbled open the pajamas, baring her chest. Deep scratches raked from her collarbone to her breast. Bruises purpled around holes where Spike's claws had pierced her skin. The wounds burned and throbbed. Her chin felt as if she'd been punched.

Behind her Spike's growling rose and fell.

She swallowed hard. Her throat ached as if she'd been punched in the larynx. She leaned toward the mirror and lifted her chin.

Finger impressions encircled her throat.

BUCK MET DESI in the parking lot. When her frantic call awakened him, he offered to go to her place, but she begged for his address. She sounded on the verge of panic, barely coherent. She parked the Subaru and he opened the car door. Her eyes were huge. He hustled her out of the cold and into his first-floor apartment.

With a cop's eyes he took in her bruised, bloody face, glazed eyes, tangled hair and the fact that she wore her coat over pajamas. He wanted to kill whoever did this to her. He guided her to the sofa, hunkered before her and took her hands. They were ice-cold and shaking.

"What happened, honey?" he asked. "It's okay. Talk to me."

Her teeth chattered. "He tried to kill me."

It took every ounce of willpower he possessed to not leap into action. He forced himself to stay where he was, to keep her looking into his eyes, and to keep his voice calm. "Who tried to kill you?"

"The gardener." She blinked rapidly and her gaze came into focus.

He rose and nearly pounced on the phone.

"Who are you calling?" she cried.

"I'm calling this in. He might still be in the neighborhood. I need a description, honey. Did you see his face?"

She leapt off the sofa, nearly tripped over the coffee table and grabbed at the phone in his hands. "He didn't have a face!"

He caught her before she fell.

"It's the ghost," she gasped. "The ghost tried to kill me." She gulped. Her hands, though small, had strength and clutched his biceps in a painful grip. "I couldn't move. I was paralyzed. He choked me and I couldn't fight, I couldn't do anything. He was black, just black, like looking into a bottomless pit. Spike attacked me—or attacked the ghost. It broke his hold."

Her chin was inflamed, turning dark with a

bruise, and bore unmistakable animal bites. He guided her to a bar stool and hoisted her onto the seat. She struggled for normal breathing, but the shaking continued unabated.

He unzipped her coat. Beneath it she wore a fleece pajama top printed with snowflakes and penguins on ice skates. The top was streaked and splotched with blood.

"Let me look, okay?" Gently, he unbuttoned the top two buttons and eased back the fabric. Deep, bloody scratches crossed angry red flesh. "I'm taking you to the emergency room."

"I don't need a doctor! It's just scratches."

"You need a tetanus shot. Maybe antibiotics." He ever so gently touched her chin, examining the bite wound. Knowing how much it hurt her, he winced in sympathy. "Animal bites are nasty. They cause infection. You have to—"

He stopped when he saw them. Five distinct marks darkening her throat. Three on one side, two on another, they were, without the slightest doubt, finger impressions.

"Shit," he breathed. "No ghost did this. Damn it, Desi, someone was in your house."

She slapped his hands away and clutched the pajama top closed. "It wasn't a man! It wasn't human. I swear to God, it was not a person." Her eyes brightened with unshed tears. "You have to believe me. Say you believe me."

He looked around for her guardian spirit. He was

now convinced it was the spirit of her grandmother who'd died only a few years ago. She wasn't here. Nameless fear turned his guts to ice.

"I believe you, honey. But you really should go to the emergency room. That's a bad bite."

"Don't want to," she said, sullen. Her shaking eased. "I hate doctors. Besides, Spike has bitten me before. They never got infected."

He sighed. "I have a first-aid kit. At least let me clean those."

She slumped, miserable and pale. Then, nodding, she worked off her coat. Her top pulled, exposing the swell of her breast where deep scratches inflamed her flesh. Buck led her to the bathroom. He had her sit on the vanity, next to the sink. He brought out the first-aid kit, a bottle of hydrogen peroxide and several towels.

"You should take off your shirt. This is going to be messy." He forced a smile. "I won't peek."

A trace of color brightened her cheeks.

He opened the medicine cabinet and picked up a bottle of over-the-counter pain relievers. "I'll get you a glass of water."

He fetched water from the kitchen. When he returned, she sat shirtless and holding a towel to her breasts. Her bare back, revealed in the mirror, was delicate with fine bones and sleek muscles covered in flawless skin. It hurt his heart to see the extent of her injuries. The scratches were concentrated on her chest, but she had them on her shoulders and upper arms, too. Spike had pulled a real cat-o'-nine-tails on her body.

She swallowed two tablets, drained the water glass and sighed.

"Let's start with your chin," he said.

She tipped her face far back and closed her eyes. Other than a small gasp when the hydrogen peroxide first touched, she didn't make a sound. There were two deep punctures, but he suspected that her traumatized flesh would bruise over her entire jaw and half her face before healing was complete. He worked antibiotic cream into the bites. A single tear trickled from the corner of an eye.

"You can cry if you want," he said. "I would."

"I never cry," she whispered through clenched teeth.

"Never?"

"Never."

He bandaged her chin and moved on to her throat. The finger-shaped bruises creeped him out. He'd had a few physical encounters with entities. Once he'd ended up with wicked claw marks on his back. Where a thin scar remained as a reminder of the encounter. Twice he'd been knocked down, and several times he'd been slapped hard enough to leave welts. He easily imagined the terror Desi must have felt to have ghostly hands strangling her. There was nothing in the first-aid kit that could treat the bruises, so he moved to the scratches.

He cleaned them first with hydrogen peroxide then set to work with a washcloth and antibacterial soap. Most were surface scratches, but there were several puncture marks that dotted her skin with purplish-black spots. The worst scratch raked diagonally from her collarbone to her breast. The end of it disappeared beneath the towel.

She held her head high, eyes on the ceiling. "So what do you see?"

"A woman who should be in the ER, getting this properly treated."

"I mean ghosts. What do you see?"

"Oh." He had to scrub where the cat's claws had opened her skin. Cords stood out on her neck, making him feel like a total jerk for hurting her. "Depends. Sometimes shadows, sometimes a glow. If they notice me or want contact, they show themselves. Some look as real as you or me."

"Full body apparitions?"

"Not often. A face, or hands. I see a lot of hands. Or they show me things that were important to them in life. The only thing I'm ever positive about is whether they're male or female. Don't know why, but that's the way it is."

"I heard you call them guardian spirits."

"The nice ones. They hang around because they're worried. At least that's my best guess. Somebody is troubled or needs assurance. I've heard people say their guardian spirits show up in dreams."

It amused him at how comfortable he felt talking about it. Since he'd met the people of Rampart he'd talked more about the paranormal than he had in his entire life.

"And the bad ones? What do they look like?"

He blotted her skin dry, then set to work with the antibiotic cream. "Black…just black. No features, no real shape. I try not to look at them. It's better if they don't know I can see them."

"Why is that?"

His chest tightened and he forced himself to focus on the scratches. "They can use people to do things. They hurt people. Tell me if I'm hurting you."

"I'm okay. What do you mean they use people? Are you talking about possession?"

"Could be." Ugly memories crowded his head. The line between good guy and monster was so very thin. "If a Dark Presence did this to you, we have to stop it."

"Ya think? How do we do that?"

"The only way I know is to figure out what they want. Since this one wants to choke you I don't think that's a plan."

"It doesn't want me. It wants Veronica. I read about the murder. How do we convince him I'm not Veronica?"

The question took him aback. Spirits weren't omniscient, but they had information they didn't have in life and they knew what loved ones needed. It troubled him that a murderous ghost could mistake a living woman with a woman who'd been dead more than a hundred years.

Maybe Dark Presences were insane. An ugly notion.

"Uh, honey, those scratches...the towel."

She looked down at her ravaged chest. She squeezed her eyes shut and dropped the towel. "Just do it."

He was a cop rendering first aid, he reminded himself sternly as he saw her breasts. A single scratch arced across one breast, slicing through the delicate pink areola. Grimly refusing to allow thoughts about how full and beautiful her breasts were, he cleaned the scratch and rubbed in antibiotic cream. Her nipples hardened under his touch, and he nearly lost it. His face actually ached with the repressed urge to kiss away her pain.

He put bandages on the deeper scratches, then stepped back. "Finished." He hated how choked and adolescent he sounded, and how relieved he felt when she covered herself. "I insist you get a tetanus shot."

"I insist I don't. I had to get one last year after I took a header off a hiking trail. I'm up-to-date."

He picked up the bloody pajama top. "I'll get you a shirt." He fetched her a sweatshirt from his bedroom and left her alone to get dressed. He went to the kitchen to make coffee.

When she joined him, she looked waifish in his oversize sweatshirt. Her face looked as if she'd gone a few rounds with Mike Tyson.

"Okay," he said, "this is what we're going to do. I go on duty in an hour. I'll ask my sergeant for some personal time and I'll go check out your house. I want to make one hundred percent sure that you didn't have an intruder. If so, I'll call in a report. If not, I'll go to work. We'll figure out what to do about Mr. Nasty this afternoon."

"Okay."

"You can stay here if you want."

"I'll go to Gwen's place. Will you feed Spike for me?" Her lower lip trembled. "I blamed him at first. I was pretty mean. But he saved my life."

"I'll take care of Spike. Coffee will be ready in a few minutes. I need to get dressed. Do you need anything else? Ice pack?"

"I'm good."

She looked miserable. And scared. Very, very scared.

Uncertain, uneasy and wishing her grandmother was here, if not to reassure Desi, then to reassure him, he left her.

In the bathroom he cleaned up and put away the first-aid kit. He stripped out of his sweatpants and T-shirt and stepped into the shower. He was reaching for the faucet when he heard her scream.

"You phony son of a bitch!"

He snatched a towel to wrap around his waist and rushed into the living room in time to see the front door slam. He tore the door open. Desi glanced at him from the parking lot. Even in the predawn darkness he felt her blazing rage. She got into her car and peeled rubber out of the parking lot.

He stood at the open door until his skin began to freeze. Then slowly closed the door.

His gaze landed on the coffee table. His insides did an elevator drop.

Scattered across the table was the information he'd found online about the deaths in her family. He'd been snooping. He'd been caught.

Knowing said he'd committed an unforgivable sin.

DESI KNOCKED on Dallas's door. She rang the bell then knocked again. Finally he opened the door.

She'd caught him in the middle of a workout. He wore cutoff sweatpants and a sweaty T-shirt revealing heavily muscled arms, and he was barefoot. His skin was flushed and shiny with sweat. He looked more like an athlete than a computer geek. And he looked very surprised to see her.

"Oh," she said. "I interrupted you. I...should go."

He waved her inside. "Rather talk to you than the weight machine. What's the deal? You look like—" his gaze raked her top to bottom "—hell."

As if she needed the reminder. Afraid to go home, she'd gone to her sister's apartment over the antique store. Gwen had been shocked, flustered and frustrated by Desi's running around town in her pajamas and her unwillingness to talk. Desi had turned up her robe collar and clutched it closed to conceal the bruises around her neck; she dismissed her bitten and bruised face as a minor argument with her cat. Desi had finally exclaimed, "Shut up! No more questions! I have to figure this out!" Gwen had looked hurt by the outburst, but Desi was too upset and frazzled to do anything about it. She'd promised to tell Gwen everything in the morning. She'd spent a few pain-filled hours on a sofa in Gwen's cluttered apartment. After borrowing a pair of jeans, with the legs rolled so she didn't walk on the bottoms, and a sweater, she'd sneaked out while Gwen was busy in the store. She kept her coat on now to conceal her braless state.

Dallas invited her to find a seat. His living room looked like Mission Control, with multiple computers strung together and an array of monitors. Books and papers were piled everywhere. She followed him into the kitchen.

"Buck is a fraud," she said. "He's been playing us from the beginning. Boot his butt to the curb."

Dallas had opened the refrigerator. He stood still, watching her.

"He has a dossier on me!" Her lower face felt like a gigantic toothache, throbbing with every heartbeat. Her chest felt feverish and sore. She'd already taken enough painkillers to sour her stomach.

"A dossier?"

Whether a few newspaper articles and obituaries counted as a dossier was open to debate. She still knew what she knew.

"He found articles about my parents and the drunk driver who murdered them. And he had Grandma's obituary. It's one of the oldest scams on

the books," she said. "He's no better than that guy
who convinced Gwen that the ghosts of Mom and
Dad wanted her to invest in his—" She made air
quotes with her fingers "real estate ventures. He
took her for over fifty thousand before I stopped it."

Watching heat creep up Dallas's neck and the
flush on his face turn dangerously hot gave Desi
some satisfaction. He closed the refrigerator.

Desi couldn't count the number of phony
psychics who had tried to convince Rampart they
were for real. Some of them concocted elaborate
ruses in their quest to gain enough credibility to take
their sleazy shows on the road.

"How do you know he has a dossier?" Dallas asked.

"I saw it in his apartment." Her hot face grew
hotter. "Nothing is going on between us. I was there
because of special circumstances. I saw it."

"You searched his place?"

The question caught her off-guard. Buck had
known she was coming. For a clever scam artist to
leave incriminating evidence lying around seemed
pretty stupid.

"Does it matter?"

"He's for real, Desi. I'm convinced of it."

"Because he made a lucky guess about a life insurance policy? Come on, Dallas!"

Dallas rubbed his jaw with his fingers. Finally he
reached past her and picked up a wallet from the
counter. "Do you know what's in here?"

"Am I supposed to?"

"Nobody is supposed to."

He brought out a quarter and handed it to her. It looked odd, strangely white, though everything else was the same. It took a few seconds to realize it was silver, rather than sandwiched with zinc and copper. It was dated 1955.

"Uncle Dave was my dad's baby brother. He was only eight years older than me. I have four sisters, so he became my big brother. My best friend. He showed me how to negotiate baseball card trades and shoot a BB gun. He helped me build my first computer. I was a pesky little kid, but he never told me to get lost."

Desi rested a hip against the counter. Dallas had never talked about his personal life with her before. The sorrow behind his story touched her.

"When I was seven, I got hit on my bike. A car plowed into me. Threw me about fifty feet. Everybody said it was a miracle I survived. Head injury, busted legs and arms, torn liver. Dave never left my side. The nurses got so sick of him hiding from them that they gave up and let him stay." He stretched a hand toward her. She put the quarter in his palm and he closed his fingers over it. "Dave said the quarter was magic. Said it was guaranteed to make my head better and it would make me walk again. He had this long story about it coming from the mysterious East and being owned by a sorcerer. A bunch of crap, but I was seven." He shrugged. "I believed. And I got better. Everything healed

without a hitch. In six months I was back in school
without so much as a limp."

He looked at the quarter as if he wanted to give
it a kiss before he slipped it back into the wallet.

Desi swallowed the lump in her throat.

"It's not something I talk about. Nobody knows
that story. Buck zeroed in on it."

"He did a reading on you?"

"It wasn't a reading like I've ever seen. I refused
to give him any clues. I don't think I said a word.
All of a sudden he got this funny look on his face
and he was looking at something none of us could
see. Then he said a guy was with me and he wanted
me to look in my wallet. He wanted to make sure I
still had my lucky 1955 quarter."

Desi swallowed against the pesky lump again.
"Dave passed away?"

"He was a Marine. He died in Afghanistan. If Buck
had collected a dossier on me, he would have known
that. He might have somehow figured out Dave and
I were close. No way in hell could he know about my
quarter. It's all on video, Desi. Buck is for real."

Dallas's tale killed the indignant fire in her belly.
All the certainty she'd felt before she knocked on
Dallas's door now whimpered away.

"Now are you going to tell me what happened to
your face?" He opened the fridge again and brought
out a bag of ground coffee.

She touched the bandage Buck had applied with
such tender care. Her heart ached. "Cat bite."

He busied himself making coffee. "If you wanted to bitch about Buck you could have done that on the phone. What's really going on?"

"My house is haunted."

He stilled, watching her without turning his head.

She drew a deep breath. "My house is haunted. I have a ghost and I want it gone."

Dallas snorted a laugh. "Now who's scamming who?"

"I am not kidding." She hooked her fingers in the collar of the turtleneck sweater and tugged, exposing the bruises made by phantom fingers. "It tried to kill me. I need your help."

Chapter Eight

Desi found herself in a position she never, in a million years, thought she'd be: The subject of a Rocky Mountain Paranormal Research Team investigation.

Dallas and Ringo blanketed her town house with infrared cameras, night-vision digital cameras and digital audio recorders. They checked and re-checked electromagnetic fields with the EMF meters and K2 meters. They looked for cold spots with digital thermometers that could detect temperature changes as small as a hundredth of a degree. Dallas even set up his new thermal camera so it focused on Desi's bed.

While the men handled the technical side, Desi sat in Pippin's downtown office. Desi recalled every possible indicator of paranormal activity in her house. Pippin documented every word. The more Desi remembered, the more the truth came clear. When she had accused Buck of causing the para-normal activity, it was because she'd been shaken by the thermal video of the reading. The more she talked, the more she realized there was a definite connection.

The ghost in her house did not like Buck Walker.

Pippin put down her pen and shook a cramp from her hand. She'd filled four pages.

"I talked to Buck," Pippin said.

Desi looked away. What Buck had done was sneaky and underhanded. If he wanted to know about her past, he could have asked.

"He told me what happened," Pippin continued, her voice low and melodious. Her therapist tone, designed to soothe. "He told me everything."

"He's a con artist, Pip. Did he tell you he dug up information about me? I don't know how he did what he did with the thermal camera, but researching a victim is the oldest trick in the book."

"He didn't dig up info about you."

"My parents, my grandmother. Same thing."

Pippin shook her head. "You have a guardian spirit. Buck wanted to know who she is."

Desi pondered whether to laugh, yell or storm out. Or give in to the yearnings of her aching heart.

"I don't have a guardian spirit. Why would I?" A spot between her shoulder blades turned cold and itchy. She refused to turn around to see if anyone was there.

"You'll have to talk to Buck about that." Pippin leaned forward and patted Desi's knee. "He cares about you, honey. A lot. He wouldn't do anything to hurt you."

"I'm not hurt. I'm mad!"

"All I'm saying is, talk to him. Let him explain before you write him off."

"Did you talk to Buck?" Dallas asked. He and Ringo had wrapped up the investigation and cleared out the equipment. Since neither man reported any experiences, Desi suspected they weren't going to find anything after reviewing the video and audio.

With her arms crossed Desi looked around her living room and kitchen. It looked the same, but it didn't feel the same. It had been invaded. Her mouth soured and her legs quivered with the urge to beat it out of there.

"I have nothing to say to him," she said.

"He told me why—"

She held up a hand to stop him. "I don't have a guardian spirit."

"Huh. You *are* close-minded."

"I am not!" She clasped her throat. This morning the bruises had been purplish-black surrounded by ugly green and yellow. Common sense said if a ghost could strangle her, then it was possible for her to have a guardian spirit. Still, the hurt and anger lingered. Buck should have asked her what he wanted to know instead of snooping around about her losses.

"Whatever." Dallas pulled on his coat. "I'll let you know if we find anything."

THE DOORBELL STARTLED Desi. Everything startled her these days. She had to work, so she spent her days at home, but when the sun lowered over the mountains and the gloom settled, nervousness got the better of her. She spent nights at a nearby motel, where she slept fitfully with a light and the television on.

She wanted her house back.

Buck Walker stood on her front porch. He held a bouquet of daisies like a shield. She drank in the sight of his broad shoulders, dark hair shining in the sun and warm, brown eyes filled with heart-melting hopefulness. Her insides lightened and her knees went weak.

He eased the flowers toward her. "Peace?"

"What do you want?"

"Five minutes." His smile touched her soul. "Please?"

She unlocked the storm door and let him in.

She snubbed the flowers and he set them on the breakfast counter, along with a pink box wrapped with a gold cord. "What's that?"

He looked good in a University of Colorado sweatshirt and jeans. Too good. His masculinity, his sheer sexiness messed with her head.

"Macaroons," he said.

She struggled to contain her surprise. There was no way in hell he could know macaroons were her favorite sweet treat. Unless he'd talked to Gwen. Why not? It seemed he'd talked to everybody else she knew. He was an annoyingly persistent man. She hated feeling flattered.

"I talked to Dallas," he said. "If you want me to quit the team I will."

She fiddled with a thumbnail. Her nails were a mess from chewing on them. She was a mess in general. "Just tell me the truth, okay? Just tell me why."

A squeaky *meow* greeted Buck. Spike did a slinky rub around the man's legs, begging to be picked up. Buck did so. "Hey, big guy. You're quite the hero."

Desi pulled a face. Spike still hadn't forgiven her. With her piling on the insults by leaving him alone in the house at night, he'd been giving her the cold shoulder.

"How's your chin? It looks better."

"No infection. So? What do you have to say?"

He put the cat down then held out his hands, palms up, in surrender. "I was wrong. I shouldn't have checked out your past. I apologize."

"So why did you?"

He rubbed the back of his head and slid his hand over his neck. He shifted his weight from foot to foot. "You have a spirit. A lady. I thought it might be your mother. She doesn't look like the newspaper photo of your mom, though. This spirit is older and has light hair. She wears a lot of jewelry. She reminds me of Gwen."

Desi caught the edge of the breakfast counter. A vivid memory filled her. Her grandmother laughing while Desi and Gwen raided her jewelry boxes.

Gwen piled on the jewels until she sparkled from head to toe while Desi made pictures on the floor out of strings of beads and rhinestone brooches.

Desi shook away the memory. All her photographs were neatly arranged in albums and stored in the back of her closet. Buck had never been alone in her bedroom long enough to find any pictures of Grandma. Gwen, however, had dozens of family photographs on display. Had Buck been to Gwen's apartment? Jealousy sliced through her like a hot, dull knife.

"I should have told you," Buck said. "She's your guardian spirit. She's been communicating with me."

Desi refused to look over her shoulder to check if her grandmother was standing in the living room. "Did you talk to Gwen? Go to her apartment? Did she show you pictures of Grandma?"

He blinked, openly puzzled. She caught her lower lip in her teeth.

"No," he said. "I got the impression you don't want me talking to Gwen about the paranormal."

She didn't want him talking to Gwen, period. Her sister was too attractive.

At the silent confession. Desi's face grew hot. She was turning into a jealous shrew over a man she didn't even know she could trust!

"The spirit is beautiful," Buck started to explain. "Classy. Sense of humor, too."

Which described Grandma perfectly. Feeling stupid, she asked, "Is she here now?"

"No. She popped in on me this morning. She's worried about you." He grinned, sheepishly boyish. "I thought about wearing my Kevlar vest. I bought flowers instead."

"You're scared of me?"

"Terrified." His smile melted her anger and hurt.

A thread of resentment lingered over Buck getting to talk to her grandmother while Desi hadn't even realized Grandma was hanging around. Feeling grief, she picked up the bouquet of daisies and held them to her nose. They smelled of greenery and springtime, reminding her of the special milled soap Grandma had used. Grandma had died in her sleep. A brain aneurysm, unnoticed, undiagnosed and ultimately deadly, all the more shocking because Grandma had been exceptionally healthy and fit.

"You can call her," Buck said. "She'll probably come if you do."

No. Losing Grandma had been devastating. Only taking care of Gwen, for whom Grandma's death had been a double whammy, had kept Desi from falling apart. Gwen's fiancé had died barely three months before Grandma did. Gwen had been such a wreck Desi had handled everything from the funeral to cleaning out Grandma's house to probating the estate. She couldn't bear to feel such awful grief again.

"I—I don't want… I need to think about this."

"Are you still mad at me?" He shifted his weight.

Anxiety darkened his eyes. Her answer mattered to him.

She mattered to him.

"You…" She fiddled with the flowers. "You hurt my feelings."

"I know. What can I do to make it up to you?" His smile made her want to sigh. "I'm not above groveling."

Now there was an interesting image. Rather than Buck on his knees, his hands clasped in supplication, she preferred him on his knees while kissing her senseless. Him naked while kissing her senseless. Embarrassment pinged her. Since when she did she obsess about seeing a naked man? She shoved her face in the flowers to hide her blush.

"I can take you to dinner. Anyplace you want."

Like his place? So she could lick honey off his naked belly?

She blurted, "Can you read minds?"

"No."

She had to look away to keep from laughing. "Dinner would be nice."

"Early dinner? Six?"

Dessert later. *Naked* dessert.

"Sounds good."

He raked his fingers through his hair while he nodded. "Do you like Thai? There's a place on Academy with killer green curry. Spicy."

"I like spicy." One more minute and she was going to ask him to get naked. "Six it is. But right now I have to get some work done. I'm glad you came over." She lowered her eyes. "I don't like being mad at you."

"Can't say I care for it myself." He placed a hand on her shoulder. "So we're good?"

"Yes."

"All right. See you at six." He looked reluctant to leave and she eased him toward the door. They should have at least one date before she asked him to get naked.

After she closed the door behind him, she fanned her face.

Almost as nice as the sudden case of hot pants was the safety she'd felt with Buck. Maybe her repeated commands to the ghost to get out of her house had worked. She moved cautiously to the middle of the living room and stood listening. The only things she heard were kids laughing outside and the hum of the computer fan.

Crinkling cellophane made her jump. Spike crouched on the breakfast bar, his face buried in the daisies. The sheer normalcy made her laugh out loud.

Maybe she'd sleep here tonight.

Maybe she wouldn't sleep alone.

THE DOORBELL RANG and Desi pulled on a robe. Didn't it just figure? The one time she was running late her date had to be punctual to a fault. She opened the door. Buck arched a brow at the sight of her terry-cloth robe.

"Am I early?" he asked.

It figured, too, that he looked incredible. Black jeans, black boots, and a supple black leather jacket over a cream-colored crewneck sweater. Right on time and gorgeous. Nervousness fluttered in her belly. She usually didn't care what men thought of her since she was so busy ferreting out their flaws. But Buck Walker was perfect. What if he nitpicked at her?

"I need five minutes." She invited him in. "I promise. Five minutes."

She hurried upstairs. She'd already showered, fixed her hair and applied makeup with plenty of time to spare. She'd even managed to cover the bruises on her face. With a bit of extra glam on her eyes, she doubted anyone would notice the scabs on her chin. She'd pulled on her best black slacks, but then the clash of the sweaters had begun. She had tried on at least half a dozen sweaters, and none looked right. She'd settled on a brown turtleneck and was in the midst of figuring out how to pull it on without wrecking her makeup when Buck arrived. Now she deemed the brown too dowdy.

She hung her robe on a hook. *Think. Think!*

Desi closed her eyes. If she weren't so flustered, she'd laugh at how ridiculous she acted. It was only a date. She was a grown woman, not a sixteen-year-old. She'd been on plenty of dates and this one was no different. She had a turquoise-colored, cowl-necked sweater in soft chenille that would cover the scabby scratches on her upper chest. And it wouldn't wreck her makeup when she pulled it over her head.

She opened the closet door. It looked wrong, but it took her confused mind a few seconds to figure out what exactly was wrong. She frowned at the bar. Instead of a row of skirts, sweaters, slacks, blouses and dresses, she saw naked clothes hangers lined up like soldiers. Slowly she lowered her eyes to the pile of clothing on the closet floor.

HATRED AND JEALOUSY struck Buck like a blast of superchilled air. He staggered back and caught himself on the kitchen counter. At his feet Spike, who'd been rubbing his jeans and meowing to be picked up, puffed up, flattened his ears and hissed.

A shadow figure blocked the light from the sliding glass door. Featureless, hulking, it absorbed light, a man-shaped black hole eating light and energy.

Buck's throat felt frozen. His muscles quivered and ice filled his torso. His feet were blocks of cement. Hatred pulsed from the Dark Presence. It buried him, swallowed him as sure and inexorable as quicksand.

Spike leaped onto the counter. Ears flat, eyes black, and every hair on his big body standing straight up, he hissed and spit. He let loose a rising *mwaroah* that any man or beast would recognize as *I will kill you!*

The shadow swallowed itself and disappeared.

Desi screamed, "Buck!"

He raced for the stairs, jumped over the three steps leading to a small landing, and took the remaining stairs three at a time.

Right before the top he struck an invisible wall that knocked him back. He caught the railing in one hand as his boots slipped on the carpeted stair. To save himself he flung himself forward, striking his knee on the stair. He kept his hold on the railing, wrenching his shoulder but stopping a fall.

"Buck! Oh my God! Are you hurt?" Desi grasped his arm. "What happened? Are you okay?"

His fury matched that of the Dark Presence's. No stupid ghost was going to push him around. He untangled his feet and rose. Desi, her eyes round and scared, seemed unaware that she wore only a bra and slacks. The bra was plum-colored and silky, uplifting luscious cleavage.

He had enough wits about him to know if he called attention to it she'd put a shirt on. That would be that.

He choked back the urge to tell her he'd been ambushed on the stairs. She was upset enough. He'd tell her later. "I'm okay," he said. "I heard you scream."

"It's back! That obnoxious son of a bitch is back!" She grabbed his hand, hauling him up the stairs behind her.

She pointed a shaking finger at the bedroom closet. "Look what he did. My clothes. He knocked everything to the floor."

He rubbed his chin, worried and at a loss. This was too much like the other time he'd acknowledged a Dark Presence. That one had been powerful, too, almost destroying him. Spirits drew energy from natural sources in order to manifest or to manipulate objects. They absorbed energy, too, from human emotions. Fear and panic, grief and loss, even great joy, could give spirits enough juice to make themselves known. There was a lot more power here than there had been in the Moore house.

"You have a lot of clothes," he said stupidly.

"Only because I haven't thrown anything away since the ninth grade." Then she noticed her state of dress and clamped her arms over her bosom. "I am not in the habit of flashing guys." She put her back to him and grabbed her robe.

"I don't mind," Buck said. The light moment winked away. "You have to get out of here, honey. This thing is dangerous."

She clutched the robe lapels. "Brilliant deduction, Sherlock. I thought it was gone! It's been quiet here. Nothing has happened. I was going to sleep here tonight!"

Her temper was up and fire brightened her eyes.

"It's me," he said, knowing he'd nailed the answer. "I'm drawing it out because it doesn't want to share you. I talked to it at the Moore house. It's as aware of me as it is of you. Jealousy drove it to murder Veronica. Jealousy is fueling it now." A low buzz filled his ears. He worked his jaw, as if to pop his ears against a pressure change. His thoughts tangled and he forgot what he meant to say.

She touched his arm. "Buck? Are you okay?"

It squeezed him. The black entity battered him, surrounded him as if seeking entry through his pores. Fear pummeled him inside as the darkness pummeled him from without. He wanted to tell Desi to run, flee the house, but paralysis gripped his throat, shaded his eyes and turned his vision gray.

"Buck!" Desi shook him. "You're scaring me. Stop it!"

He wrenched against the coldness and staggered. Desi tried to catch him and they both stumbled against the wall. He pinned her. The smell of her inflamed him. He saw her scent as dancing swirls and curlicues in tantalizing colors. He grasped her face in both hands and kissed her. Hard.

She struggled and shoved at his chest. Her mouth was hot and oh, so sweet. He wanted her so badly. He wanted to devour her, become one with her, take her and own her and make her his own forever.

Mine. You're mine. None can have you save me and you're mine and I will have you and none other.

At the sound of that menacing voice—was it his?—Buck shook himself. As if pulling his arm through quicksand, he pushed his thumb up under his jaw, striking the sensitive gland. He jammed it with as much force as he'd use against any criminal trying to fight. White pain rocketed through his head and down his neck. He fought through it and forced himself away from Desi.

Before him Desi slid slowly down the wall. Staring up at him with shocked eyes, she racked in air and clutched her throat. Buck stared at his hands. Hands that had tried to strangle the life from her. Hands that had not belonged to him.

Moaning, he rushed from the bedroom, stumbled down the stairs and fled the house.

DESI FOUND BUCK in the parking lot. He sat in his Jeep with the door open. He leaned his face on his arms folded atop the steering wheel. Desi approached warily.

"Buck?"

When he lifted his head, she saw his eyes were dark with anguish and his face looked pale in the yellowish interior car lights. She stood tensed to run, studying his face, seeking any sign that he was not himself. His misery drained away her fear and she touched his shoulder.

He thrust his cell phone at her.

"Call 9-1-1," he said.

She refused the phone. "What? Why?"

"I assaulted you. You have to report it."

Dumbfounded, she thought about what it would mean for him. It wasn't that long ago that a law had gone into effect that every person, male or female, convicted of domestic violence lost all rights to own or carry a firearm. A police officer without a weapon could not be a police officer. She licked her bruised lips. She was surprised none of the neighbors had called the cops about the ruckus in her house.

"It wasn't you," she said.

"Like hell it wasn't." He flipped open the phone. "I'll call it in."

She grabbed for the phone. Though his arm was too long for her to reach the phone, at least he couldn't dial the number.

"Listen to me! It wasn't you in there. I swear to God, Buck, it was not you!" She stared into his eyes, willing him to believe. His arm relaxed and he dropped the phone on the passenger seat.

"All my life I've felt crazy," he said. "Even when I saw spirits that were friendly and helpful, part of me wondered if I had a chemical imbalance or some weird kind of epilepsy. Or maybe it *is* schizophrenia. All my life I've been weird, out of place, seeing things and knowing things I shouldn't. Maybe I'm psycho instead of psychic."

"It wasn't you," she said. She stroked his cheek. "It wasn't even your face. It's like…it was like a mask! It was the ghost. I know you wouldn't hurt me like that. I know it."

"Do you?"

She wanted to crawl onto his lap and hug him until the anguish left his face. "Don't you know by now that I'm an unforgiving bitch? I carry grudges. If I thought for one second that you tried to hurt me, you're damned right I'd be on the phone to the cops." Fury tightened her forehead and made her guts ache. How dare that monster take something beautiful and make it ugly? She glared at her front door. "That wasn't you in there. I saw his face. It wasn't you. I want him out. I want him gone. You have to help me."

"I'm the reason he's attacking you. He's jealous."

She snorted. "So a ghost gets to choose my boy-friends? I don't think so."

Buck perked up a bit. "Boyfriend?"

"You know what I mean," she mumbled, her cheeks hot.

A car pulled into the small parking lot. Here she stood in her robe and slippers. Her neighbor gave her a funny look. She gave him a little wave.

"We have to talk to Dallas." She drew a deep breath, shoving down the fear. This was her house, her property, her life. "I'll meet you at his place, okay?"

He rose from the car and caught her arm. "Don't go back in the house."

"I have to. I'm not staying the night, but I'm not running around town in my robe. Wait if you want. I won't be more than five minutes."

"Desi—"

"It's okay! I'm wide-awake and ready for him. You wait out here for me." She forced a big smile and left him at the car.

For all her bravado and righteous indignation,

opening her front door was one of the hardest things she'd ever done in her life. Sweat chilled her forehead. Every hair stood on end. A flock of quarrelsome birds took up residence under her rib cage. She jerked open the storm door, shoved open the front door and marched inside. The air was thick and sour, and every step felt like wading through mud.

"Spike?"

No answer. The door to the basement was closed, but her reserves of courage were thin and she could not make herself open the door.

She grabbed her purse and cell phone. Clutching the leather bag like a shield, she eyed the stairs.

One, two, three…*run!*

She pounded up the stairs and into her bedroom. At least her recent stay in the motel meant her overnight bag was already packed. She threw in some clean underwear and a pair of jeans. She turned for the closet and turned away. She could not make herself step inside to rifle through the mess for a sweater. It was too easy to imagine the ghost slamming the door behind her and having her alone in the dark. Instead she snatched up the brown sweater from the bed and pulled it over her head.

A querulous *meow* startled her.

"Spike?" It sounded as if it came from under the bed, but checking would mean getting on her hands and knees and putting herself in a most vulnerable position.

Things hid beneath beds.

"If you want to go with me, get your butt out of there. I don't have time to chase you." She slipped on her shoes then waited for the count of ten to see if the cat would show. Horrible guilt washed through her, but not even that could make her look under the bed. At least Spike had proved he could handle himself against the ghost. She grabbed her purse, overnight bag and coat, and hurried out of the bedroom.

The atmosphere was so heavy, breathing hurt. She filled a large bowl with water, and for good measure filled the sink, too. She set out several bowls of kibble, hoping Spike didn't make a pig of himself and eat it all in one night. She hurried to the front door and pulled it open.

She spun about. "This is my house, damn it! You're dead. Veronica is dead. I don't care what happened a hundred years ago! Get out of my house. You don't belong here! Go away! Get out!"

Her nerve broke and she fled.

Chapter Nine

Buck and Desi met Dallas at Rampart headquarters. Without a houseful of people to generate body heat the apartment was cold. Dallas saw to the comfort of his computer equipment rather than the comfort of people. Desi kept her coat on.

"I was about to call you when you called me," Dallas said. "I caught something on video at your place."

Desi's heart sank. No more, she begged the powers that be. No more paranormal crap for her frazzled mind to deal with. Buck wandered restlessly, glancing at the display of horror-movie posters and framed Victorian séance photographs.

"Ringo and I are still going over the video and audio." Dallas looked at his wristwatch. "Man, that cute chick must be working at the deli tonight. Ringo has been gone forever." He patted his flat belly. "He's supposed to be getting sandwiches."

Desi focused his attention on her problem. "What did you find on the video?"

Dallas studied Buck. Dallas was far too scientifically curious about the paranormal to get upset about anything his investigations uncovered. Desi had seen him startled, stricken by claustrophobia and pushed around by spirits. His reaction was always "This is cool!" Desi wondered what it would take to scare Dallas.

Seeing a monstrous face superimposed over Buck's? It had sure scared the snot out of her.

"You first," Dallas said.

Buck stopped pacing. Desi had trouble catching his eye. She thought she understood. He was the law, he served and protected, and at his core he was a gentle soul. No doubt the attack shook his entire image of himself. Desi wished Pippin were here to talk to him, to assure him that he wasn't a monster and he certainly wasn't dangerous. Pippin had a gift for that sort of thing.

"I assaulted Desi," Buck said.

"It wasn't you," Desi said. She told Dallas what had happened with her closet then the monster taking over Buck and trying to strangle her. "The face. I saw a face on top of Buck's face." She closed her eyes, trying to remember, though she didn't want to remember at all. "It was like a mask. A mask made of Jell-O. Almost, but not quite transparent and sort of…jiggly. Shifting. Its eyes…" She shoved her icy hands into her coat pockets. "They were black, all black. Like bottomless pits."

"Wish I'd been there with a camera," Dallas said. He flinched away from Desi. "Sorry! That's what I do. Even you have to admit that's really cool. What did you see, Buck? What did you feel?"

"I saw it downstairs first," Buck said.

Desi shot him a wondering look. He hadn't told her that.

"A shadow. No real shape, just blackness. When Desi screamed and I ran upstairs it tried to block me. Then it shoved me down the stairs."

Dallas pulled out a chair, turned it around and straddled it backward.

Buck's gaze turned distant, troubled. "I felt paralyzed. Like I was wrapped up like a mummy, or trapped in quicksand. I was moving, but I couldn't move. Does that make sense?"

"Not really, but go on," Dallas said.

Buck touched his thumb beneath his jaw. "I jabbed myself. Pain broke the hold." He licked his lips. "I heard it talking in my head. It thinks Desi belongs to him."

"Sounds like demonic possession," Dallas said. "Do you feel anything right now?"

Before Buck could answer, Desi said, "It wasn't *in* Buck, it was *on* him. It thinks I'm Veronica Skillihorn. This is no residual haunt and it's definitely intelligent. It means business." Remembering how she'd pooh-poohed Mrs. Moore's claims of being strangled made Desi feel mean and stupid. She should call the woman and apologize. Then she'd call a Realtor and list her house for sale. "I never meant to invite it home. That was so stupid!"

"Stuff happens," Dallas said.

"It doesn't happen to you," she said bitterly, slumping on the chair. "I never should have joked around like that."

"You're not totally to blame," Buck said. "I know better and I still confronted it. It doesn't matter. What matters is that it focused on you and it knows it can use me to get to you. Do you think Alec Viho can help, Dallas?"

"It's possible, but the weatherman says a storm is coming that could be winter's last hurrah. Supposed to hit later this week. Alec might not want to risk the drive down from Wyoming. I'll give him a call and we'll see how his schedule looks. Alec runs a boot camp for bad boys. Hard for him to drop everything." Dallas drummed his fingers on the chair and stood up. "Want to see what we caught at your house?" he asked Desi.

"Not really, but I guess."

She and Buck followed Dallas into the tech room. Dallas dropped onto a chair then typed commands on a keyboard. Humming, watching the screen, he clicked through commands until he had a video image isolated. "Haven't cleaned it up yet. But you can see it. This is your bedroom, Desi. We had the IR camera mounted on the dresser, focused on the bed. Watch the corner. It happens fast." He tapped a key.

Desi and Buck leaned in to watch the computer

screen, which showed her bed in a black-and-white video. A shadow appeared in the corner, mushroomed into a conical shape, then collapsed and vanished.

Desi's stomach did a slow roll.

Reports of the phenomena stretched back through history and were a fixture in folklore and ghost stories. They were called shadow people, shadow men, shadow folk, wraiths, Death, succubi, incubi and Hat Man. In folklore they were considered ghosts clinging to a traumatic event, perhaps one the shadow man caused while alive, or they were demons summoned through occult practices. Ever since the Roswell UFO incident a cult of believers had risen who believed shadow men were aliens.

Scientists and skeptics said shadow men were a result of people misinterpreting shadows caught in their peripheral vision, or they were nightmares in a state of waking sleep called hypnagogia. Chemical poisoning or sensitivity to high electromagnetic fields accounted for many sightings. There were even seizure disorders that could cause people to see shadow men.

Not so easy to explain were the increasing number of shadow men caught on camera. No camera in the world could photograph hallucinations.

Desi swallowed a sour taste in her mouth.

"Dark Presence," Buck said. "That's what I see."

The overhead lights dimmed and the computer monitor flickered. Dallas snapped up his hands if to protect his electronic darlings from a power surge.

After a few seconds, Dallas said, "This makes for an interesting situation. The entity is obviously intelligent and interactive. It responds to stimuli. It manipulates the physical world."

Desi slugged his shoulder. "I don't want to study it, Dallas! I want it gone. It has to be Veronica Skillihorn's killer. If I remember correctly none of the newspapers reported him saying anything at the trial. Maybe he couldn't. I bet he doesn't even speak English. Maybe he needs to say he's sorry."

Dallas nodded. "Yep. Strangling you is a good way to do that." Desi reared back to slug him again but stopped when he waggled a finger at her. "Maybe we should take a direct approach. Contact it. Ask it what it wants. What do you think, Buck?"

Buck frowned at something behind Desi. She glanced at the door.

"The lady is here," he said. "Do you mind if I talk to her, Desi?"

She exchanged a look with Dallas. He was grinning. "Uh, sure," she said. "Where is she?"

Buck pointed with his chin to a spot to the right of Desi. "Is your name Mary Hollyhock? Are you Desi's grandmother?" He nodded. "Hi. Did you see what happened at Desi's house earlier?"

Desi stared where Buck said Grandma was. She saw nothing. Not a shimmer, not a glimpse, not so much as a change in temperature. Desi strained to hear, strained to feel. Nothing came to her, and grief hurt her heart.

"Ma'am, I can barely see you. Can you come closer? Did you see what happened?" He cocked his head. "Do you know why it wants to hurt Desi?" He shook his head and turned his hands palms up. "I don't know what that means."

A lightbulb winked out. Dallas made a pained noise.

"We're supposed to go there? Will it be there? Okay. I get it. It can't go there." He blinked at Desi as if bringing her into focus. "She's afraid of the Dark Presence."

"Where does she want us to go?" Desi was fairly certain she did not want to know.

"Evergreen Cemetery."

THE NEXT MORNING Buck and Desi, each driving their own cars, arrived at Evergreen Cemetery. They parked at the main office. When they met, Buck wanted to hug Desi, to kiss her, but he held back. If he understood Mary Hollyhock correctly, the Dark Presence could not come here. He sensed no invader waiting to pounce. Even so...

He handed Desi a pocket-sized canister of pepper spray.

"What's this?" She peered at the small print outlining its use and effective range.

"If Jell-O Face shows up, give him a snootful. That stuff can stop a bear."

"Grandma says it can't come here. Isn't that what you said?"

"Better safe than sorry." He looked around at the cemetery.

Evergreen had once lay on the eastern outskirts of Colorado Springs, but the town had some built up around it. It was still the largest in town.

"Where are you going?" he asked, when he saw Desi walk away.

She nodded toward the office. "To find out where Arturio Carpetti is buried. That's why we're here, right?"

He spotted Mary Hollyhock. He could see her clearly from head to toe. She wore tan slacks and a fitted blazer. Her rhinestones sparkled. She beckoned. Buck took Desi's hand. "This way."

Mary led them south, cutting a straight path through the cemetery. The ground grew hillier, the trees taller, the brush thicker. Dates on headstones slipped back in time.

Desi hopped off a rock wall and slid on the grass. "Should have worn hiking boots," she said.

"Uh-huh," Buck said. He removed his sunglasses to better see Mary. He squinted against the sun. It was around forty degrees, and the sky was unbroken by clouds. The pleasant weather was temporary. A warm day or two always preceded late winter storms.

Desi said, "I bet you see a lot of ghosts right now."

"I rarely see spirits in cemeteries." He searched for Mary. Instead of walking or floating, she flitted, her image appearing and disappearing, always moving south.

"You don't?"

"Only if they're hanging around somebody alive. The spirits I see are attached to people or structures. I don't think they're interested in their bodies."

"Gwen will be deeply disappointed to hear that." Amusement softened her face. "She loves ghost hunting in cemeteries. Her dream vacation would be Paris so she could explore the catacombs." She slipped again. This part of the cemetery was a slalom course of small hills and hummocks and stone-retaining walls.

Buck took her hand to help her up a hill. "Are you going to clue her in?"

"I honestly don't know. It doesn't matter what kind of proof I show her, she still believes the world is swarming with ghosts. She's wrecked her life because of it."

"She seems happy to me."

"She's a financial mess."

"Maybe money doesn't matter to her. She's looking for something bigger, something with meaning."

"Not falling for every charlatan who comes along would be meaningful."

He sensed in her a deep-seated fear. Maybe it wasn't concern about her sister that drove her to explore the paranormal. Maybe her own belief that people were nothing more than meat sacks doomed to a short life and then nothingness terrified her. As much as she resisted the idea of an afterlife, she actually wanted it to be true. Coming face-to-face with a ghost had to be short-circuiting her entire belief system.

"Have you ever considered that educating her would help? You don't want me talking to her, but why—" He stopped when he saw Mary appear behind a monument. She rested both hands atop the granite.

Skillihorn.

The name was carved into polished granite on a chest-high block of stone. In a Classical style to look as if Greek columns supported a portico, the monument was larger and more ornate than the nearby headstones and monuments. To the right was Veronica Skillihorn's headstone.

Desi read, "Veronica Eugenia Skillihorn, Beloved Wife, Angel on Earth, Angel Now. Born 1874, died 1898." She sighed. "She was only twenty-four. Is this what Grandma wants us to see? Where's the gardener?"

Buck crouched on the left side of the monument and eased back winter-dead grass. The grave marker was a simple rectangle of rough, gray stone engraved with Charles Skillihorn's name and the dates of his birth and death. He'd outlived his young wife by one year.

"That's bizarre," Desi said, looking between

Veronica's headstone and Charles's marker. "He was a wealthy man. Why the cheap stone?"

Buck rose and stepped back so he could take in both graves and the monument.

Grandma materialized over Skillihorn's grave. A brief appearance and one he'd miss if he'd blinked. He saw enough.

"What? Why are you smiling?"

"You asked if seeing spirits helped in police work. Actually mothers, or mother figures, help. They don't like it when their kids misbehave. If I run into a group of juveniles and know one of them is guilty, all I have to do is look for a pissed-off female ratting him out."

"So why is that funny now?"

"Mary ratted out Skillihorn. He murdered his wife."

"But they convicted the gardener. They hanged him."

Prejudice against immigrants and Skillihorn's standing in the community probably made Carpetti an easy target. "Skillihorn framed him."

"What does Grandma want us to do?"

Buck drew a blank. The murder had happened in 1898. Anyone connected to the crime was dead. Anyone who even *cared* was dead.

Desi crossed her arms and looked up at him. "You're the cop. How do we investigate this and clear the gardener?"

Buck laughed. He really wanted to kiss her. She was so fierce, so sexy. "I'm a patrol officer, not a detective."

"What's the difference?"

He'd never felt the allure of making detective. He liked the hands-on aspect of his job. He liked helping people, being in the middle of action and preventing crime. It seemed to him that detectives were always playing catch-up. "Training," he said, though it was more than that. "I know a detective who's into cold cases. I can talk to him. But I can tell you right now that as interesting as this is from an historical perspective, no way is it a police matter."

"But... Oh. I guess it would be a waste of time. Can't arrest a ghost. So what do we do?"

He looked around for Mary. He wished she could talk. It was frustrating as hell playing charades with spirits. But she was gone. Apparently she'd used up her energy bringing them here.

He put his arm around Desi's shoulders. He liked the way she fit so perfectly against his side. He stilled, listening with his inner ear. They were alone among the dead. He kissed the top of her head, drinking in the sunshine smell on her hair. She leaned against him.

He studied Skillihorn's ugly gray marker. "That has to mean something. He spent a lot of money on the monument and Veronica's headstone. He must have cancelled a headstone as fancy as Veronica's. Why would he do that?"

"Maybe his heirs saved some money and went cheap on the stone."

Buck gave her a dry look. "I don't think so. A wealthy man like him would have had a marker as fancy as his wife's. Uh-uh, looks like guilt to me."

She made a skeptical sound. "Yeah. Guilty. So he shows remorse by strangling me?"

"We'll figure it out."

"We better do it fast." She showed him her game face. "I'm not losing my house to a ghost. I have a business to run and people who depend on me."

Buck couldn't believe he once thought the ideal woman was soft and sweet, needing a big, strong man to kill spiders and shield her from the harsh realities of the world. Desi Hollyhock drove home why such women bored him. With her feisty independence and hardheadedness, Desi wouldn't tolerate being treated as a child or taken for granted. She squished her own spiders and met life head-on.

She was sexy as hell, but not easy. Desi would never be easy—for man or ghost.

"Why are you looking at me like that?" she asked.

He touched her cheek with a knuckle. "You have the most beautiful eyes I've ever seen."

Her mouth softened and the corners curled. "Is Grandma watching?"

"Could be, but I don't see her. Why? I think she likes me."

Desi walked her fingers over his jacket and smoothed the lapel. "Of course she does. You're a man. She was worse than Gwen when it came to setting me up. Queen of the blind dates." Her eyelids lowered and the faint smile disappeared. "She died in her sleep. No warning at all. It was a brain aneurysm. I'd just bought my house and I was busy fixing it up. She wanted to help decorate, but I kept making excuses. She loved stuff. The bigger and gaudier it was, the more she liked it." She sighed. "I should have let her help me. I could have changed it later. It would have made her happy."

"I'm sorry you lost her, honey." He cupped her face with a hand and she closed her eyes, leaning into it. "So I'm just a man, huh?"

She smiled, her eyes still closed, and made a musing noise.

Tough cookie.

He touched her lips with the lightest of kisses. As alluring as she might be, necking in public was not his style. When he removed his arm her brief expression of disappointment pleased him.

"Investigating the murder is probably a waste of time," he said. He pointed at the weathered grave marker. "We should look at what happened afterward. He's got unfinished business, so let's figure out what he was doing before he died."

"And finish whatever he started? Sounds like a plan, I guess." She sighed heavily. "First I have to go home."

"You can't do that, honey."

"I don't have a choice. I have to take Spike to Gwen's. It's not fair to leave him alone that long. Besides, he'll get mad and eat my furniture. And I need my laptop and files. I have clients. I don't think they'll be sympathetic about a ghost. I'm not going to stay, but I do have to take care of things."

An offer to accompany her lodged in his throat. He was the catalyst for Charles Skillihorn's insane jealousy. Accompanying her might lead to anther encounter. "I don't want you going alone."

"No worries there. I'll call Pippin and see if she can go with me."

He couldn't bear it. He swept aside his inhibitions, pulled her into a tight embrace and kissed her until desire threatened to overtake him and he had to let her go.

DESI PUT THE KEY in the lock with a trembling had. "I really appreciate this, Pip," she said. "It's ridiculous, and I'm sorry—"

"If you apologize one more time," Pippin interrupted, "I will smack you. We're friends. It's an honor to help you out."

Desi turned the key and the deadbolt clacked. Her belly churned and her throat tightened with phantom pain. No fear, she warned herself. She pushed the door open and strode inside.

Spike meowed, sounding annoyed. He nearly tripped her while curling around her legs. She scooped him up and hugged him. He meowed and grunted, and rubbed his head against her chin.

Pippin petted the cat and cooed over what over a pretty boy he was. Spike began to purr. When Desi set him down, he stuck so closely that every step was a challenge. She turned on lights as she went, and tensed for bulbs to blow. She turned on the computer.

"What do you need me to do?" Pippin asked.

"Um, I need some things from the basement." With everything working and the cat acting normally, Desi relaxed a little. She led Pippin downstairs and pulled out a suitcase, portable file box and cat carrier.

Pippin picked up the suitcase. "So tell me about you and Buck. Other than the ghost thing, how—"

Desi whirled on her friend. "Shh! Don't say his name. Don't even think about him!" She held her breath, waiting for a black mass to loom in her face or for the washing machine to blow up.

"Sorry," Pippin said. "Oh, sweetie, I'm so sorry. I hate seeing you like this."

"I hate it, too. My chest hurts and my stomach is upset. I'm having trouble sleeping. This is driving me crazy. All I want to do right now is run screaming out the door."

"Then let's get out of here. Come on."

Upstairs, Desi put Spike in the carrier right away, before he remembered now much he hated the carrier. He rattled the mesh door. Next she transferred data from the computer to a thumb drive. Anger rose in her as she thought that now she'd have to work at her clients' businesses instead of her home. The damn ghost had invaded her house, forced changes in her work habits… It took a mighty effort to not start screaming at it. Instead, she loaded the paperwork she would need into the portable file box and made certain the power supply for the laptop was in the carrying case. Then they went upstairs.

Desi packed underwear and toiletries. Drawing a deep breath, her knees shaky, she opened the closet door. The sight of naked hangers and all her clothes on the floor charged her nervousness once again. She took excellent care of her belongings. Even as a child she'd been tidy and careful. For that damned ghost to fling her stuff around made her clench her teeth.

She found the clothing she wanted to take, then began hanging sweaters, blouses and skirts where they belonged.

"Desi? Desi, come look at this." Pippin said. "That is creepy,"

Desi stepped out of the closet.

Squarely in the middle of her bed was a long, narrow depression in the shape of a person stretched out on the comforter. It was as if a man were taking an afternoon nap.

Rage exploded within her and she rushed the bed. She snatched up a pillow and beat the mattress, pounding the man shape. "Get out! Get off my bed! It's mine! Get out! Get out!"

"Desi!" Pippin grabbed her arm and hauled her away from the bed. "Desi."

Desi dropped the pillow. She'd pounded the comforter askew and knocked several pillows onto the floor. There was no sign of the depression now.

"You're all packed," Pippin said. "Let's get out of here. Let's go."

A light bulb blew with a *pop*.

"Now." Pippin dragged Desi toward the door.

Chapter Ten

Desi lugged the cat carrier up the stairs and into Gwen's apartment. Her sister met her with a raised chin and disapproving eyes.

"I'm mad at you," Gwen said.

"What did I do?" Desi put Spike on the floor, but hesitated about letting him out of the carrier just yet. Her nape prickled. Her sister was angry. For all her theatrics Gwen wasn't given to yelling, screaming or heated arguments. When she got angry, she got quiet.

"First you show up at my place in the middle of the night, looking like you were mugged. Now you need me to watch Spike. But you don't tell me anything?"

Desi looked down.

Gwen continued. "You snuck out before we could talk. If you think for one second I don't know you're avoiding me, you're out of your mind." She spoke in a low, calm tone. She was really mad.

"I'm sorry, Gwen. There's…I'm having…I've got a lot on my plate right now. If you don't want to watch Spike, I'll take him to a kennel."

"It gets old," Gwen said. "You treating me like an idiot." She crouched and opened the cat carrier door. The big yellow cat stalked out, past Gwen and into the middle of the living room. He looked around as if wondering if he liked the place, or perhaps he considered redecorating. Every surface was covered in antique linens, glassware, Asian ceramics and vintage metal toys. There were plenty of things for him to move around.

"I'm sorry you feel like that," Desi said. "That's not my intention."

Gwen held up a hand. "Don't you dare say you're protecting me." She turned around and headed into the kitchen. "Come on, Spike. I'll get you some milk."

Desi perched on the edge of a Georgian settee. Its tufted velvet upholstery and ornately carved camel-back made her think Spike might be better off at a kennel after all. Even if he refrained from using his claws, the velvet would act as a magnet for his hair. Gwen's apartment had ten-foot ceilings, carved and fluted woodwork, and there was barely an inch of wall space showing between paintings in antique frames, tapestries, hand-painted china plates and other artwork. It was an angry cat's paradise.

The apartment made Desi feel claustrophobic. Gwen's anger made the feeling worse.

"I forgot his accessories," Desi called. "I'll run to the store and get him food and stuff. Unless you want me to take him someplace else."

Gwen stepped out of the kitchen. "I'm mad at you, not Spike. *He's* more than welcome."

Desi winced. She supposed she deserved that. "Things are complicated right now, Gwen. It doesn't have anything to do with you."

"You're right. I have my life, you have yours. We're not joined at the hip or anything. If you don't want to talk to me, no law says you have to."

Desi closed her eyes, struggling with her own anger. The last thing she needed was a fight with her sister. Her conscience urged her to tell Gwen about Grandma. Spill everything about the ghost and Buck and how very frightened she was. But she didn't want to drag Gwen into it. Didn't want Gwen to worry or get involved or insist on probing Buck's psychic brain cells.

As she rose, her gaze fell on a photograph of their grandmother. It was a fanciful head shot with Grandma wearing her biggest rhinestone earrings and a diamond-like collar. Grandma had taken her and Gwen to a glamour portrait store in the mall. They'd spent a ridiculous, laugh-filled afternoon getting made up and their hair teased. Grandma and Gwen had convinced Desi to pose with a feather boa. Her throat tightened at the memory.

Gwen broke into her thoughts, "I've been dreaming about Grandma."

Desi gave a start. She picked up a Venetian glass bird and turned it in her hands, pretending to look at it.

"For the last three nights I dreamed about her. She's so real, I can almost smell her perfume. I can almost touch her."

"What happens in the dreams?"

Gwen canted her head and narrowed her eyes. For a moment she looked just like Grandma with an intelligence even brighter than her beauty. "She's telling me to take care of you. It's weird, isn't it? You always take care of me. She says you're in trouble and I need to help. Are you in trouble, Desi?"

"Dreams are just neurons discharging in your brain," Desi said. Her throat hurt with the weight of the lie. "It doesn't mean anything." Under Gwen's scrutiny Desi wanted to squirm. She tossed her sister a bone. "I need to go. I have a date with Buck."

Gwen brightened. "Really? Is he the problem?"

"Sort of." Desi set the bird down and pretended to examine other knickknacks on the table.

"So what's wrong with him? He doesn't floss regularly? His socks don't match? He talks about old girlfriends?"

"Am I that bad?"

Gwen nodded. "You're horrible. I'd say if you don't want him, I'll take him, but I hate leftovers." She smiled. "So what is his deadly flaw?"

Other than trying to strangle her? She slipped a hand in her coat pocket and touched the cold canister of pepper spray. It wasn't that he gave it to her, but that he honestly meant for her to use it if she had to. Burn him, blind him, anything except let him hurt her. She wondered if it made her a bad person to consider his twist on self-sacrifice sexy. Probably.

"There's absolutely nothing wrong with him."

"Ah ha! That scares you." Gwen looked at the cat carrier then back to Desi. "Are you going out of town with him? Is he taking you skiing or something?"

Dang it, Desi thought. Why hadn't she thought of that as a cover story? She lifted a shoulder and tried to look mysterious.

"Oh my God! Why didn't you tell me? Where are you going?" Gwen scooped up Spike and cuddled him against her shoulder. "Ooh, has your mommy been playing naughty with the sexy cop?"

"Oh, stop. I don't know how things will work out between us," Desi said. "He's special. I don't want to tempt fate by saying too much. I really do appreciate you taking care of Spike. I'll be back in a bit with food and a kitty box."

"Don't worry about it. I have to run to the store anyway." Gwen set the cat down and gave Desi a big hug. "Oh, sweetie, I don't know what to do about you. You deserve a nice man. Especially one as hot as Buck. He's a good kisser, right? You wouldn't be this upset if he had a worm mouth. Great kissing covers a multitude of sins."

Desi wriggled out of the embrace. She untangled Gwen's beads and necklace and picked a few cat hairs off Gwen's vintage cashmere sweater. "I need to figure some things out. Then we'll talk. Okay? I promise."

"I'll ask Grandma. She always had good advice about man troubles."

Desi left the apartment and went out the back way to the tiny lot where she'd parked her car. Jealousy made her kick a few rocks. Buck got to see Grandma, Gwen got to see Grandma, and all Desi got was a badass ghost trying to kill her.

DESI HURRIED toward the entrance of East Library. The wind had seriously picked up and the coming storm was boiling out of the north. The clouds were low, as black as night. The thin glow of the sun setting over the Front Range, like the tail end of a retreating army, made the sky look even blacker. A few years ago a spring storm had shut down the city with three feet of snow. Trees downed, power lines broken, people trapped in vehicles and homes, the interstate closed. This storm looked like it might be even worse than that. A gust of wind tore at her coat and whipped hair into her face.

She recalled every novel she'd ever read or movie she'd ever seen about people trapped in a spooky mansion, or in a mountain cabin, or on an island while being menaced by a killer. Her imagination piled snowdrifts against the doors and windows, and shut off the electricity. In the dark and the silence with no one to hear her scream while a Dark Presence materialized in a corner and its gelatinous face took form.

A shudder wracked her.

She rushed to the library door and engaged in a tug of war with the wind to get the door open. The warm, bright, bustling library made her shudder again, but in relief. She ran her fingers through her hair. The coffee kiosk was closed, but the smell of coffee and spicy chai lingered. Hunger tapped her. She had better get to the grocery store this evening and stock up on some food before the storm hit.

She visited the ladies' room to comb her hair and fix her makeup before she went looking for Buck.

The library was crowded. The check-out lines stretched beyond the guide ropes and snaked into the magazine racks. Every card-catalog computer terminal had a user. Most people, when thinking about Colorado Springs, thought of Pikes Peak, Garden of the Gods and mountain sports. Desi always thought of books. Along with the main library downtown, the Pikes Peak Library District had at least a dozen branches, plus a bookmobile. There were several major bookstores that were always busy, and every grocery store had entire aisles devoted to books and magazines. It was a bibliophile's kind of town.

She'd have to pick up some books in case she did end up snowed in at the motel.

No horror novels, though.

She headed to the computer stations that offered Internet access and saw Buck seated before a terminal.

She paused a moment to drink in the sight of him. He leaned back on a plastic chair, his long legs stretched beneath the table and his hands laced over his chest. As handsome as he was, his attractiveness went far deeper. He projected an air of calm strength, of dependability. One look into those brown eyes and it was evident he was a man of his word, a man who took his responsibilities with grave seriousness.

She grinned, amused at thinking his psychic ability was actually okay. Everybody had little quirks.

He looked up and smiled at her.

The rest of the library and all the people and noise faded, leaving only Buck. Desi sighed and made her way to the computer terminal.

"Hello there," he said, and slipped an arm around her waist.

"Sorry I'm late," she said. "I had to take care of some clients."

The computer screen showed Internet search results for *exorcism*. The sheer number of entries raised her eyebrows. Either a whole lot of people found themselves in her type of predicament, or folks really liked the subject.

Buck eased her closer to him. He looked around to see if anyone paid attention, then pulled her down and pecked her lips.

The kiss wasn't enough. She kissed him again, this time savoring the sweet firmness of his lips and the heady aroma of his skin. He tightened a hand on her waist. When he parted his lips and teased her with his tongue, Desi pulled back.

Being banished from the library for lewd and lascivious behavior wouldn't do.

He rose, looking around. "Here, take this chair."

She added "gentlemanly behavior" to the list of things she adored about him.

She waved him down. "Sit. I'm okay."

"Are you?" he asked. "Any problems at your house?"

A chill slithered down her spine. "He was there. It looked like he was napping on my bed. There was an actual depression on the mattress. Pippin saw it, too." She refrained from mentioning her temper tantrum. No sense embarrassing herself with the details.

"Did you find anything?" she asked. She wrinkled her nose at the computer screen. "Exorcism?"

"I don't think we want to go there. It's morbid. Dangerous, too. Exorcists seem to do as much damage to the possessed as the demons do. Besides, the Dark Presence doesn't get inside me." He scowled distantly, his brow furrowed in concentration. "It's like that kid's game where you grab somebody's arm and smack them with their own hand. It's like I'm a tool, or a puppet. I don't see how an exorcist can help with that."

He logged off the computer. "I can see why you get so upset about quacks and scammers. A lot of people are making big money off exorcising ghosts and demons." He picked up a yellow legal pad from the computer desk and took her hand. "Let's find someplace to talk."

They hadn't taken two steps before a girl with spiky hair claimed the computer station.

Buck led Desi toward the rear of the library, past the nonfiction stacks.

She asked, "Have you ever been tempted to go into the paranormal business?" She felt stupid as soon as the words were out. She knew Buck well enough by now to realize he had no interest in preying upon people's fears or mental instability.

He showed no sign of taking offense. "I've helped a few people figure out why their guardian spirits hang around. But not for money. It's private."

Something in his tone touched her heart. She couldn't begin to imagine what it must be like to see things no one else could see, and to know things he had no business knowing.

They found a pair of unoccupied reading chairs.

Wind rattled the building and howled against roof vents. Buck said, "It's going to be a bad storm. The duty sergeant already called me. I'm on standby right now."

The upholstered chairs were low and soft, positioned so the corners of the arms touched. Buck held her hand and his boot touched hers. Desi studied his hand. Long, strong fingers and square nails. She imagined him naked. Long, lean, muscular, his skin hot. She blinked the image away.

What in the world was wrong with her? Such pre-occupation with sex wasn't like her at all.

She asked, "So did you find out anything else about Skillihorn?"

"Nope. I spent an hour with the research librarian. After the murder trial Skillihorn disappeared from the public eye."

"How did he die?"

Buck shook his head. "Don't know. I called Tara and asked her to see if she can find anything else. She has found some more information about the house's history." He tapped the legal pad. "She's quite the bulldog when it comes to research."

"That's Tara," Desi agreed. "Never satisfied with a little bit of information. She has to know it all. If anyone can find out what Skillihorn was doing before he died, she can."

"I also talked to MacGregor. He's the detective I told you about. Likes cold cases. I told him a friend was researching a book and wants to know how to go about reopening an old murder investigation."

"Anything useful?" Desi tried to not look where he stroked her palm with his thumb. It sent tingles up her arm, through her body and settled into a case of hot pants.

"He said you have to go back to the beginning, start over as if the crime just happened. Visit the crime scene, reexamine all the evidence, interview all the witnesses and figure out what was missed the first time."

"Well, that's helpful."

"When I told him the crime happened in 1898, he laughed at me."

"Can't imagine why." Even as she chuckled, the mental wheels churned. Dreamy images of Buck interfered. Did psychic ability increase his sex appeal? She pulled her hand away from his. "Ghosts have unfinished business, right?"

Now he moved his foot slowly up and down against hers. Even that turned her on. She tucked her feet tightly against the chair.

"That's been my experience," he said.

His crooked little smile said he knew exactly the effect he had on her. She kept her eyes fixed on the wall, but peeking at him in her peripheral vision proved irresistible. Her cheeks warmed.

"It's actually an assumption," he said. "Some spirits don't want anything to do with me at all. Others seek me out. Those who do have unfinished business disappear once it's finished. I like to think they're free to join their loved ones on the other side."

Sadness washed through her. She wondered what her grandmother wanted, what unfinished business she could possibly have. Desi feared she was the unfinished business holding Grandma in limbo.

"Can't you ask Skillihorn what he wants? You said you can hear him talk."

Amusement drained from his face. His chest hitched. "You don't understand."

She turned on the chair to face him. That night at the Moore house he'd refused to return indoors. At the time she'd attributed it to his being spooked by a haunted house. His fear went much deeper, though, perhaps even deeper than her own.

"It's too dangerous to contact it. It can make me do things." He sounded bleak. "I can't risk letting it use me to hurt you."

Desi veered off that trail. She pointed at the legal pad. "Did you find anything useful?"

"This is from talking to Tara." He lifted a page and shook his head. "It's all about the house. Looks like Skillihorn has been making trouble for a long time. His brother sold the house not long after his little boy died. Then the bank took possession. That's been the pattern. Bought then abandoned time after time. For a while the city owned it and they gave Colorado College a long-term lease for student housing. The college broke the lease after a few years. I assume students refused to live there. It's gone as long as twenty years without anybody living in it."

Desi snapped her fingers. "Jonathon! You can talk to Jonathon. He's friendly. He coexisted with his uncle in that house for a long, long time. I bet he knows what Skillihorn wants."

His eyes sparkled and his mouth twisted.

"Are you laughing at me?"

He hooked a big hand behind her neck and drew her face within inches of his own. "Shh, this is a library."

She whispered. "You're laughing at me."

He chuckled. "I'm thinking about this cute girl I met not so long ago who told me ghosts are bunk."

She sought the truth about the paranormal, but the truth she found wasn't what she expected or wanted. She supposed that was pretty funny. "You think I'm cute?"

"Adorable." He kissed her nose and turned her loose. "We can't talk to Jonathon. Alec says he's gone. And I refuse to attempt calling him back. Sorry."

"Why? I mean, I didn't know you could do that, but why wouldn't you?"

"He's a little kid. He spent too many years alone. It's not right to bring him back. It's cruel."

"Oh." Desi had to think about that. Was it cruel for her grandmother to hang around? Cruel to drag her into this mess because her granddaughter stupidly invited a ghost to follow her home?

He patted her shoulder. "We'll do what we can. If all else fails I'll see if I can lure Jonathon back. But that's our last resort. I don't want him lost in the corporeal world when his family is over on the other side."

A faint buzz caused Buck to take his cell phone off his belt. He checked the number and said, "Dallas." He answered.

Desi drifted on her own unhappy thoughts. After Desi's parents had died, Mary Hollyhock had taken in her and her sister. No questions, no hesitation, not a second thought about how it curtailed Mary's love of travel and put a damper on her social life. Grandma had given her all to raising Gwen and Desi. Kind, loving, smart and involved, Grandma had made sure her granddaughters lacked for nothing. Now Desi prevented Grandma from going over to the other side.

Buck closed his cell phone. "Dallas has a plan. He says if we pick up some pizzas and take them to his place, he'll tell us all about it."

Desi groaned. "Dallas loves this stuff too much. I just know I'm going to hate his plan."

Laughing, Buck rose and extended his hand.

She took it and stood. "You know whatever he has in mind involves cameras."

"No big deal. You're photogenic."

She stuck out her tongue. "I'm going to grab some books first. If I get socked in by the snow, I need something to read."

She moved quickly through the shelves of fiction, judging books by their covers, the sexier the better. If she couldn't see Buck naked, then a racy novel or two would have to do. He waited for her to get through the check-out line. He smirked a bit at her choices, but said nothing as they walked into the cold wind.

Halfway across the parking lot, Buck stopped dead. "Wait a minute. What do you mean?"

Desi saw he wasn't talking to her. "What is it?"

"Your grandmother wants us to go back to the cemetery."

"What? Why? What is she telling you?"

"She showed me Veronica's headstone."

Buck laid a hand on her shoulder. "Call her, honey. Ask her if everything is all right. Something feels wrong."

A fierce wind sliced beneath her clothing. The temperature was near the cheek-burn stage. Squinting against the wind, Desi longed to see what Buck could see, to sense what he sensed. She wouldn't feel so stupid as she said, "Grandma. Grandma? Buck says you need to tell us something. Is something wrong? Please come back."

Hunched into his coat, Buck shook his head.

"Grandma? Please?"

Still nothing.

"Is she all right?" Desi asked. "You don't think she's sick or something?" Saying that made her feel really stupid. Her deepest fear was coming true— she was turning into Gwen.

"Ghosts don't get sick," Buck said. "I'm sure we're supposed to go back to the cemetery."

"Now? It's dark."

"Nice thing about cemeteries; nobody is going anywhere. Tomorrow, after I get off work. Now let's get some pizza and see what Dallas pulled out of his bag of tricks."

Chapter Eleven

By the time Buck reached Rampart's headquarters the snow began to fall. The weather report was predicting up to twenty-four inches of snow and warning people to stay off the roads north and east of the city. Buck parked his Jeep behind Desi's Subaru and followed her to the door, Buck carrying two large pizzas.

Mary Hollyhock showing him Veronica Skillihorn's headstone nagged at him. At the cemetery he'd sensed nothing from the woman's grave. Or from her husband's, either. No matter how he looked at it he couldn't see what it was about the murdered woman's grave that drove the dark thing Charles Skillihorn had become.

He smiled at Desi, trying to look more relaxed than he felt.

He looked up and down the street. Snow swirled around the corner streetlamps. There were single-family homes built in the 1970s interspersed with duplexes that all looked to have been stamped from the same mold. Every window shone with lights. Some flickered from television sets. Residents parked on the street or in narrow driveways. It was the kind of neighborhood where family disputes were usually handled quietly, burglars didn't bother and teenagers were relatively well behaved.

Nice and normal.

His body quivered with a sense that nothing was normal. Ever since seeing the image of the headstone the world had felt askew. No matter how he tried, the knowing didn't help.

John Ringo met them at the door. He smiled broadly at the pizzas and whisked them away to the kitchen.

"Hi yourself, Ringo," Desi said, with a roll of her eyes.

Buck helped her out of her coat. He glimpsed the line of her throat, the delicate curve of her jaw, and desire stirred. He wanted nothing more than to whisk her away from here. Take her to her bedroom and that huge bed. He recalled the books she had selected at the library. The title of one had the word *ravishing* in it. That was what he really wanted to do. Ravish Desi. Hold her, love her, give her everything within and without he had to give, then devote his life to finding more to give.

She turned her head slightly, her crystal-blue eyes shadowed by thick lashes. A tremulous look that made him feel bigger, more powerful. A look that made him feel magnificent. A silent laugh twitched his throat. He doubted he'd ever used *magnificent* in conversation.

"Are you okay?" she whispered.

"Sure." His unhappiness returned, deeper than ever. Before that night in the Moore house, before Desi issued her invitation, he'd thought he knew how to handle Dark Presences.

Hide. Pretend they didn't exist. Keep his eyes averted and his thoughts to himself.

Too late now. Hiding wasn't an option. Deserting Desi was completely out of the question. That thing had taken up residence in her house and it wouldn't leave on its own. A showdown was inevitable.

Dallas popped his head out of the tech room. "Hey, guys! Did you bring pizza? I'm starving."

From the kitchen Ringo called, "I'll put it on the table. Who wants a beer?"

Desi went to the kitchen. Buck headed to the tech room, where he found Tara Chase and Tony Keegan. Tara asked if the information she'd provided had done any good. Buck said, "I hope so."

He looked at a pair of computer screens Dallas had activated. Both showed sound waves. The screens were in sync.

"New software," Dallas explained. "We're trying to get it to work."

"It's for EVPs, Buck," Tony said. "You haven't had the pleasure yet of catching EVPs. Borrrring. Sometimes we'll collect thirty or forty hours of audio recordings. Then we have to go through them in real time. You sit, you listen, you try to stay awake."

"It's tons of fun," Tara said with a snicker. She had a lean, outdoorsy attractiveness, and was working on her master's degree in history. She vibrated with hummingbird energy, and Buck wondered how she stilled long enough to do the research she did. "Especially when you're listening to eight hours of an empty room."

"I'm working on software," Tony said, "to detect variations in base wave noise. I know we miss some EVPs because they're so brief or subtle. What I hope is that the computer can catch noises. It'll mark the time on the recording. That'll still mean going through hours of audio, but at least it'll give us a heads-up about where to start."

"So that's what you do, Tony? Software?"

"Yeah. Medical software. Boring compared to this, but it pays the bills."

Realization came slowly to Buck. Headquarters was very quiet, in a spiritual sense. He'd seen entities around Tara and Dallas before. Like Mary Hollyhock, they were no-shows tonight. He couldn't sense the slightest shimmer of other-worldly energy.

It had been like that at the grocery store where he and Desi stocked up on food for the coming storm. The store had been packed with shoppers, but no spirits. There hadn't been any in the pizza place, either. Buck thought hard, trying to remember. Spiritual entities to him were like the mountains. Pikes Peak, over fourteen thousand feet tall, towered over the city of Colorado Springs, but he'd lived here long enough that he rarely noticed it anymore. It was just there. Spirits were like that. He only noticed when something unusual happened.

Now they were gone. Like looking west and seeing a big hole where the mountain had been. It made him itchy all over.

"Did you talk to Alec?" Buck asked Dallas.

"Briefly. Pizza first. I haven't eaten all day."

Once everyone gathered in the main room, Tara looked out the front window and groaned.

"My car drives like crap in snow," she said. "I have to get home."

Tony pulled back the draperies, showing everyone that the snow screamed from the sky, whipped into sheets by the wind. It was sticking to the window in clots. "I gotta blow outta here, too. Dallas, my man, we'll work on the program later. Okay?"

"More pizza for me," Ringo said. He was a bear of a man with a black beard and a mop of black hair that didn't look as if it could be tamed.

Buck suspected the sloppy shirts Ringo wore disguised a mountain of muscle. As clownish as Ringo acted, he was far from simple. Intelligence blazed from his deep-seated eyes. Buck had asked Ringo once what he did in real life, when he wasn't hunting ghosts. "Butter sculptor," Ringo had said.

Tara and Tony put on coats and gloves, said their goodbyes and headed into the storm. A wicked gust of wind swirled snow inside before Dallas could get the door closed. No psychic power was needed to know Buck would be putting in a lot of overtime the next few days.

Desi and Ringo had set out the pizzas, paper plates and a roll of paper towels on the old conference table. Dallas and Ringo popped open beers. Buck took a soda. Desi wrapped her hands around a steaming mug of tea.

Buck opened his mind and listened with his inner ear. Other than howling wind rocking the apartment walls and the hum of electronics coming from the tech room, all he heard were the mundane sounds of people eating pizza. Unease made it difficult to sit. His appetite disappeared.

Dallas polished off a slice and took another. "Alec couldn't talk much. He just got in from a survival trek with his boys and the storm has already hit at his place. He has his hands full. He'll try to get down here next week, but that's the best he can do right now. He e-mailed some information." He drank deeply from the beer bottle, wiped his mouth with a paper towel and said, "Shadow Men spirits are the damned. They're intelligent and interactive, but they can't save themselves. All they can do is keep replaying whatever doomed them."

The past dragged at Buck, filling his head with ugly memories of another place, another Dark Presence.

"The definition of insanity," Desi said. "Doing the same thing over and over, and expecting a different result. So Skillihorn's ghost is insane. How do we get rid of him?"

"According to Alec, it's not easy," Dallas said. "They're vampires, sort of. They feed on human energy. They can feed on other spirits, too. Usually they're connected to a specific place, trapped there, but if they're disturbed, if they steal enough energy they can move. Native American folklore has lots of stories about traveling ghosts."

"So how do we get rid of him?" Desi sounded exasperated.

"Alec said they challenge people because they need to be defeated. They can't release themselves or break the curse that holds them. It's sort of a stop-me-before-I-kill-again thing."

"Can we communicate with it?" Buck asked. The mere thought of that drew his insides into a knot. "Ask it what it needs?"

"Alec thinks we can. The ritual requires a circle of four people. Everyone needs to be cleansed. Purified spiritually. Then it can be summoned and trapped in the circle." Dallas looked at Desi. "Everybody has to be in their right mind."

She bristled. "There's nothing wrong with my mind."

"You're a little high-strung, kid."

When she slumped in the chair, Buck patted her hand. He wasn't any happier about Alec's proposal than she was. The Dark Presence, however, wasn't going away on its own.

"We're winging this," Dallas said. "Headed into a new territory. I trust Alec knows what he'd doing. We'll get Pippin to be the fourth member of the circle. She's fearless."

Ringo nodded amiably. "She's the least nutty out of all us."

"So what's the deal with cleansing and purifying?" Desi asked. "We have to wander in the wilderness for forty days? Build a sweat lodge?"

An inappropriate image of Desi languidly naked in a steam-filled hut popped into Buck's head. He lowered his face to hide a grin.

"That's Alec's milieu," Dallas said. "How are you doing? Are you staying with Gwen? You aren't at home, are you?"

She touched her throat and gave a nervous laugh. "I'm in a motel." She glanced at the window where the wind made the glass groan. "I can hang for a few days."

Buck wondered if she'd accept an offer to stay at his place. She could have the bedroom, and he could take the couch. Or whatever.

"I just want my house back," Desi said. "I want my life back. I hate being scared. I hate jumping at every little noise." She crossed her chest with a finger. "I swear, I will never again disbelieve anyone who says their house is haunted."

Ringo patted her arm with a paw-like hand. "I knew we'd bring you around. Welcome to the dark side."

"YOU DIDN'T HAVE TO ESCORT ME," Desi told Buck.

She was glad he had insisted on following her to the motel. They were in whiteout conditions, and snowdrifts were piling up against curbs and buildings. Snowplows rumbled along the interstate and main streets, but the snow came down faster than they could clear it away. Desi's Subaru had all-wheel drive, but the curvy, hilly roads between Dallas's place and the motel made for white-knuckle driving and a lot of breath holding when SUV drivers who thought themselves invincible roared past her little car. The steady shine of Buck's headlights in the rearview mirror had made her feel safer.

At the motel her tires crunched snow in the parking lot, and she pulled into a space that she hoped put her between the lines. Buck grabbed the groceries out of the trunk and they ran to the entrance. Desi had to clear snow off the keycard slot to get the door unlocked. Once inside the hallway they stomped snow off their shoes, but they still left a trail as they walked to her room.

"It's no problem," Buck said, as he waited for her to unlock the room.

She felt a long way from home, and didn't want to be here. She hated the smell of industrial-strength cleaning products and the lingering essence of the hundreds of people who'd taken refuge here in the past.

Buck hesitated in the doorway.

"Come on in," she said, the words tangling in her throat. She prided herself on her independence and her ability to solve problems on her own. She hated being scared and lonesome. Hated facing another night in a strange bed surrounded by strange noises, and awakening disoriented and unsure where she was.

Buck came inside and closed the door. He set the bags on the floor next to a tiny table.

The room had a coffeepot but no refrigerator, so her groceries consisted of nonperishables. There was a restaurant within walking distance, but if the storm got too bad she'd settle for tuna and crackers.

"I know you have to get up early in the morning," she said. She forced a laugh. "You don't have to stay." She knew as soon as he left she'd start obsessing about cleansing rituals and mystic circles and facing the ghost head-on.

He looked around the room at a double bed, two nightstands, a dresser with a television bolted to the top, a tiny table with a pair of chairs and the requisite ugly painting featuring ducks flying onto a pond.

"I don't know why you have to stay here," he said. "This is depressing. Can't you go to your sister's? Or a friend's house?"

"Like you said, I'm a vampire. I'll be up all night working. I don't like bothering people."

He grinned. "You bother me."

She felt bad.

He added quickly, "In a good way." He lowered

his head and scuffed the toe of his shoe across the shaggy carpet. "You should be in a nicer place. This isn't a North Nevada flophouse, but it's close. I could put it on my credit card."

Torn between being touched by his offer and deeply offended, she stared at him until he lifted his head enough to see her.

"I can afford a better hotel," she said. Being touched by his generosity and concern won out. "But all I need is a bed and a table. And a coffee-pot. No sense wasting money on amenities I won't use." He looked embarrassed and she went to him, taking his hands. "That's really sweet of you. I'll be okay." Now that she touched him, she couldn't bear to let him go. "If you, you know, want to hang out a little bit, you'll see it's perfectly safe."

He tipped her chin with a gentle finger. "You look beat. I know you aren't sleeping. Even vampires need a nap now and then."

"I have a lot of work to do."

"Why? It'll run off if you don't get right to it? Trust me, it'll be there tomorrow. I'm pretty sure you won't be able to go anywhere, either. How about this? You get ready for bed. I'll hang out for a while. We can watch TV. I bet you'll fall asleep in five minutes."

Fatigue washed through her. She doubted she'd slept more than two hours at a time since Skilli-horn's first attack. Suddenly her limbs felt weak and heavy, and the strain settled in her joints, making them ache. "That would be nice," she murmured.

She went to the bathroom to change.

Her flannel pajamas gave her pause. These were pink with skiing polar bears printed on the pants and a large picture of a bear drinking hot cocoa on the shirt. "Oh so sexy," she breathed. Gwen was always trying to drag her to Victoria's Secret for fancy underwear and slinky pajamas. Now Desi wished she'd gone along. She changed into the pajamas and turned to the sink to wash up. While she brushed her teeth she began to wonder what Buck would think if she took off the pajamas and walked out naked.

She really, really wanted to see him naked. The mere thought of his tall, lean body with those broad shoulders and muscular arms made her knees weak. Imagining him touching every inch of her body, kissing every inch of her body, filled her breasts with heat. Her aroused nipples pushed at the flannel. She clutched the vanity until her knees steadied.

She rinsed her mouth and lifted her face to the mirror. Her cheeks were flushed and her eyes were overly bright. Never had she been this hot for a man. Never. She, with the eagle eyes when it came to finding flaws in a man, couldn't find a single thing wrong with Buck Walker. Not in his looks, his habits or his character.

Love is blind.

She blinked rapidly at her reflection. Love?

Where had that come from? She barely knew the man. They hadn't even gone out on a first date.

Lust? That made her wince. She wasn't ruled by passion. Never had been, and couldn't imagine ever doing so. She thought things through and acted with deliberation, after weighing the pros and cons.

She made a face at her reflection. Like now. Talking herself right out of jumping Buck's bones when all it would take would be the barest touch from him to have her mindless and moaning. She did think too much.

Compromise then, she decided firmly. She wiggled out of the pajama pants and wore the shirt, which reached midthigh, as a nightshirt. Her bare legs tingled in anticipation of his touch. Even the touch of his eyes would shoot her to the moon. Heat made her feel liquid inside. Who was kidding whom? She stripped off her panties.

Already she was wet and soft, aching and weak in her hips.

She opened the bathroom door.

She paused there, her bottom lip caught in her teeth. "Hey, Buck?"

"Yeah?"

People on the television talked about the storm. "Do you have any tattoos?"

A long pause, then a hesitant, "No. Why do you ask?"

"No reason." She turned off the bathroom light. Buck stretched out on the bed. He had one arm hooked behind his neck and held the television remote in his other hand. He had laid out his coat so his shoes didn't touch the coverlet. He'd turned back the sheets on the other side of the bed.

His gaze went straight to her legs then rose slowly. It lingered on her breasts. His nostrils flared and the notion that he could smell her arousal made her dizzy.

She needed to say something, anything, but knew whatever came out of her mouth would be idiotic. Aware of him watching her every move, she went around the bed and slid under the covers. The icy sheets made her break out in goose bumps. When he offered an arm for her to rest her head, she snuggled against his shoulder. Her chest hitched as if her lungs had forgotten how to work in tandem.

She sensed sadness around him. It was in the tightness of his fingers against her arm, in the heavy silence of his breathing.

It softened her desire and the urgency faded. The ache she felt in her heart overtook the ache in her body. "What's wrong?" she asked. "You know, other than the obvious."

"The obvious is enough, isn't it?" His low chuckle rumbled against her ear.

She knew she shouldn't keep him here, not on a night like this. His Jeep was built for off-roading, for slipping and sloshing through mud, racing through snow and climbing boulders. City streets held their own brand of treachery, especially when other drivers were involved. She watched the blue scroll bar on the lower part of the television screen. It listed school and event closures. The entire city was shutting down.

"You're in for a fun time at work tomorrow," she said.

"No doubt."

"What's wrong?"

He looked at her. "You already asked that."

"Tell me and I'll quit."

For a moment she thought he would ignore her, or laugh, or even turn his attention to the television, where the tail end of a medical drama had people in scrubs gazing fiercely into each other's eyes. "I'm sick of ghosts," he said bitterly. "I'm tired of trying to figure them out."

She smoothed her hand over his chest. His flannel shirt was soft but substantial under her palm. His chest beneath had subtle contours. She fiddled with a button, fighting the urge to fill the silence.

In the end, Buck spoke. "I never really know what they want. In a way it's kind of like communicating with animals. Body language and the expression in their eyes. Sometimes they show me things that are crystal clear. Usually I have to figure it out, like playing charades. Even the ones who can speak out loud, well, it's like listening to EVPs. I pick up a word or phrase, or a mumbling I can't quite hear."

His shoulders stiffened and his muscles turned rock-hard beneath her head. "They don't belong here. This isn't their world anymore. Some of them are so sad, so lost, I can't stand it. And I know, *I know,* most of them aren't here because they want to be here. They're sacrificing themselves for loved ones. I think something is supposed to happen once they get over to the other side. Heavenly reward, re-incarnation, who the hell knows? Mostly I can't help them. I can't figure it out. I see them, I feel them, and I know most of them just have to figure it out themselves."

She touched his face. Beneath her fingertips she felt stiff beard stubble. She traced the sculpted line of his jaw and chin. "You said you helped some of them."

"Some. Not enough. It's bad enough seeing human misery. The thing that tears me up the most on the job is a domestic dispute with little kids involved. I don't care if adults make themselves miserable. If they beat the hell out of each other or wreck their lives with drugs and drinking and acting stupid. It's their choice. But little kids are screwed. It doesn't matter what I do. Leave them and they're at the mercy of adults who are addicted to drugs or drama. Take them into custody and it doesn't matter how good the foster homes are, the kids suffer, missing their parents, knowing they aren't loved. Knowing they're just property to be shuffled around."

Desi's throat tightened and a burn began behind her eyes. She wanted to cry. She wished she could cry.

"I wish I didn't see ghosts." He exhaled in a long, heavy sigh.

She wished she knew if talking about it helped or just made him hurt more. "When did it start? Seeing them, I mean."

"Forever. Guess I was born with it. They were normal to me. I didn't talk to them when I was little. Don't talk to strangers and all that. Some of them noticed me noticing them. They waved or smiled." A trace of a smile touched his mouth. "Then I asked my mother about her father. I didn't know him. He died not long after I was born. I saw him around the house all the time. One day, when I was about five, I saw him in the kitchen with my mom. Full body, as real as she was. He wore carpenter pants and old yellow work boots with frayed laces. He was bald and his scalp had that oily look old guys get. I asked my mom who he was. She asked who I was talking about. That's when I realized she couldn't see him. She walked right through him and he didn't flinch. I said, 'Him, the bald guy with the mustache. He's standing right there.' He started showing me framed photographs. Pulling them out of the air like a magic trick. I recognized some of the pictures. My grandmother and Aunt Ellen and pictures of him, the ghost. I said, 'He wants you to put the pictures out. Quit hiding them in the closet.'"

"Wow. What did she do?"

Another heavy sigh. When he spoke his voice was hard, tight with pain. "She went ballistic. Total meltdown. That was the first time she ever hit me. Knocked me on my ass, then picked me up and spanked me."

Filled with outrage, Desi propped up on an elbow and stared at his face. His bleak expression fueled her fury. "How could she be so cruel?"

"I scared her."

She waited, and waited some more, until finally she said, "That's it? Do you still talk to her?"

"She's my mother."

"So what?"

"So nothing." He smiled and played with her hair, pulling it through his fingers and letting it fall. "I like your hair. It's so soft."

"You forgive her?"

"She is what she is, honey. I'm her only child. She wanted me to be normal. Nobody wants a weirdo kid."

She lay back down, her head against the crook of his arm, irritated by his acceptance of what she considered child abuse. "I wouldn't forgive her."

"That's you." He laughed. "You'd make a great prosecuting attorney."

"What about Dark Presences?"

He jerked as if touched with a live wire. "I don't want to talk about that."

He spoke so flatly, with such finality, her curiosity faded. She said, "I'm sorry I didn't believe you."

"I'd be disappointed if you had. I like you being so tough-minded."

"Hardheaded."

"That, too." He brushed his lips over the top of

her head. She heard him inhale, drinking in her scent.

Desire burned through her, hotter than before. She shifted her legs. Awareness of her nakedness beneath the thin pajama top was driving her crazy.

He stared at the television. The news had come on and an idiot reporter stood in the snowstorm, his voice cracking with the cold. It always made Desi wonder why reporters did that. All people had to do was look out a window to see for themselves how bad it was.

She pleaded silently for Buck to speak, to say something before she began pestering him about ghosts again. She didn't want to talk about ghosts or the weather. His eyes shifted, looking at her. He turned his head and stared into her eyes. Each breath caressed her. Inflamed her.

She couldn't stand it. "I'm not wearing any underwear."

He kissed her. Gently at first, then harder, hotter, his mouth teasing and hungry. Heat arced through her. Even her hands ached with arousal. Her blood seared her veins. He eased down the covers and pulled her closer. She squirmed, every inch of her body crying out for his touch. He stroked her bare leg and she gasped. When he slid his hand beneath her shirt, over her hip, she moaned. He kissed her senseless. She couldn't breathe. She didn't need to breathe. She needed to touch him. She clutched the back of his head, her fingers tangled in his thick hair. She kissed him and kissed him, starving for the taste of him, drowning in his heat. He pushed her shirt higher, cupped her breast, teasing the inflamed nipple with his thumb. Both of them hissed between their teeth.

She struggled away, pulled off the shirt and tossed it aside. She rolled atop him, straddling his hips, and rocked against his erection. Rough denim roused exquisite pain. He drew her down for another kiss, now rough and clumsy. He grasped her hips and caressed the tender areas above her hip bones, working his hands downward, inward, closer, maddeningly closer to the source of her heat.

She sat up, her mouth swollen and damp. She ached for his kiss as soon as contact broke. She needed to get him out of his clothes. Needed his naked body against hers. She fumbled at his shirt buttons.

He slid a hand between her legs, his fingers insistent and sure. Orgasm hit fast and hard. She threw back her head and arched her back as a cry escaped her. She rocked against his hand, cried out again when he slipped a finger inside her. She went backward, slowly, straining her thighs and opening herself wider to his blessed, beloved hand. Waves of pleasure rolled on and on, an endless tide triggered by the rhythm of his fingers plunging deep inside.

Dazed, coming back to herself, his hand was suddenly too much and she pulled herself upright.

Breathing too raggedly to speak, she eased his hand away, shaking her head. Every muscle in her body went limp. Her feet and palms tingled. Her hips were boneless and spent.

"Damn," he breathed. His eyes were glazed with heat and his smile was crooked.

Shyness gripped her and she folded her arms over her breasts. "I—I'm sorry. I don't… That's never—"

He pressed a finger wet and fragrant with her musk against her lips. "Shh. Don't even think about apologizing. You're amazing." He pulled her down and kissed her face, her chin, her throat.

Multiple orgasms? She'd heard of such things. She hoped to find out if it were true.

"Get out of those clothes, Buck. Please. I'm dying to see you naked." She worked on his shirt buttons. He wore a T-shirt under the flannel shirt, and she jerked it out of his jeans, baring a flat, muscled belly bisected by a line of black hair. She pushed the shirt up, baring the curve of his ribs and a beautiful chest. She kissed the hot flesh over his heart and imagined the strong pulse beating in time with hers. He played with her breasts and smoothed his hands over her rib cage and waist. He seemed content to let her undress him without any help. Or maybe he liked watching her clumsy eagerness. Maybe this was his secret. Tease her until she went out of her mind.

She scooted down his thighs. She was so ready for him again, she burned for him. She unbuckled his belt, unsnapped the jeans and unzipped them, and all the while he made little noises in his throat.

He helped, a little, as she tugged and twisted to get the jeans and underwear off his hips. When he sprang free she stopped, her eyes wide. "Whoa," she breathed. "Impressive."

"Thank you." His voice was low and gravelly.

She couldn't resist giving him a kiss and tonguing lightly the sensitive, turgid head that twitched beneath her touch. His grunts of pleasure made her dizzy. A little tit for tat was called for, but she didn't care that she was a selfish bitch—she wanted him inside her. "Come on, get out of these clothes. Help me."

Light flared. She let out a squeak and whipped her head about. Through a curtain of hair she stared at the television, where people in a commercial now had bright green faces and the background pulsed with insane colors. Colors shifted to the red spectrum. The volume blared; the screen went blinding white. A hot, acrid smell of burnt plastic struck her nose. The television made a terrible hissing noise and went dark.

Buck grabbed fistfuls of her hair and growled, "Whore."

Stunned, Desi slapped at his hand. He pulled her hair hard enough to hurt. "You're too rough! Stop it, Buck!"

He moaned in horror, in utter dread. He grabbed her shoulders in a crushing grip and flung her off his body.

Flat on her back, one foot tangled awkwardly in the covers, she stared at the blurry, wavering, ghostly face of Charles Skillihorn.

Chapter Twelve

Desi's mouth opened wide, but the scream lodged deep in her paralyzed throat. Skillihorn's face obscured Buck's in a gelatinous mask that feathered away at the edges like smoke. Only Buck's eyes, wide with horror, shone clear behind the murk. She ripped her foot free from the twist of sheets and blanket and fell backward off the bed. She hit hard and dislodged the scream.

The ghost lunged at her then. She kicked wildly and her heel connected with something solid.

Buck/Skillihorn grunted. She rolled, gaining her hands and knees. She scuttled backward until she struck the door.

Darkness coiled around Buck's entire body. He clutched the edge of the bed, his knuckles white and strained. The darkness pulled at him. It lifted one of Buck's arms and his fist pulled the sheet from beneath the mattress. He twisted against the darkness, dropping onto his belly, straining and groaning, fighting his own arms while that thing grappled for control.

"Hit me," Buck pleaded. His lips pulled back, baring his teeth. Darkness pulsed, pulling at Buck's arms. The mattress rose in the macabre tug of war. *"Hit me!"*

She scrambled to her feet and leaped toward the table, where her purse hung on the back of a chair. She snatched it and whirled, swinging the purse by its strap. It struck Buck's shoulder. It was like striking a boulder. His anguished eyes, barely visible behind Skillihorn's vengeful face, urged her on. She swung the purse at his head this time, and it connected with a thunk.

The dark mass shuddered and disappeared.

Buck collapsed, his face on the mattress.

She backed toward the door, groping behind her for the handle, ready to flee naked into the hallway if she had to.

Buck rolled onto his back. He clutched his head with both hands and groaned.

Desi, meanwhile, searched the corners of the room for any trace of the Dark Presence, for any shadow that seemed too black or seemed to shift. She saw nothing.

Buck pulled up his jeans. The zipper rasped, the only sound in the room. He sat up and turned his head. One eye was squeezed shut and the other watered. He stood and his hands visibly shook as he buckled his belt. "What's in that purse? Bricks?"

It was *his* face, *his* voice, but Desi remained where

she was, stricken with chills on her skin and in her bones. She felt the weight of her purse. It contained a calculator, a date book, a makeup kit, a hairbrush, a checkbook, a wallet and a library book she'd tucked in there earlier in case she got stuck somewhere.

"Honey, it's okay." He scooped up her pajama shirt and held it out to her. "It's gone."

She dropped the purse and grabbed the shirt. She pulled it over her head. Shivering began in her knees and worked its way upward. She had to clench her teeth to keep them from chattering. A red mark on Buck's chin was beginning to swell and she remembered kicking him.

"How did he get here? How?" Her voice cracked.

He sat on the edge of the bed and gingerly touched the side of his head. He looked at his fingers as if expecting blood.

"Oh God, I hurt you." She wanted to rush to his side, to comfort and apologize and tend him, but her feet were blocks of ice.

"Whapped me pretty good." He smiled, weakly. "Maybe the department should issue purses instead of nightsticks."

"Quit making jokes! This isn't funny. Where did he come from? How can he do this? It's not fair! I'm not safe in my house and now I can't even make love to my boyfriend?" She felt as close to crying as she ever had.

"I knew it."

"You knew what?" she demanded. She watched him closely, ready to snatch up the purse and hit him again if she saw any trace of Skillihorn on Buck's face. "What?"

"The spirits were gone. At the grocery store and Dallas's place. And your grandmother at the library. She showed me the headstone, but it was fast. She couldn't stay. It's following you."

She wrinkled her nose against the stink emanating from the fried television set. She had no idea how she was going to explain that to the motel staff. "I can't stand this, Buck. What are we going to do?"

"Get dressed."

"Is Grandma here? Can she help?"

He shook his head. He squeezed his eyes shut and touched his head again. "No. We have to go back to the cemetery. Skillihorn won't go there. He can't." He gave her a frustrated look. "Please get dressed. You're too damned sexy to talk to like that."

No one had ever called her too damned sexy before. It took the edge off her taut nerves. "We can't go to the cemetery. It's closed at night and we'll get arrested for trespassing." Keeping an eye on him, she sidled to the window and eased back the draperies. Snow blocked the view of the parking lot. "It's terrible out there."

He glanced at her legs and arched his eyebrows.

"Oh." She hurried to the bathroom. She started to close the door, but couldn't make herself do it. Couldn't get rid of the creepy apprehension about being stuck in a small room with a ghost. She wanted to pull back the shower curtain to see if anything lurked, but she could not make her hand touch the vinyl. She pulled on her pajama bottoms and a pair of heavy socks. She looked at her face in the mirror. Her mouth was swollen. There was a light abrasion on her cheek from whisker burn. If not for her wide, frightened eyes, she'd look like a woman well-loved.

Anger burned, rising like flames through her entire body. That damned ghost was not ruining her life. It was not wrecking what grew between her and Buck.

She straightened her shoulders and her spine.

Buck was packing her laptop computer into its case. "What are you doing?"

He looked her up and down. "I said get dressed. You can't stay here." He zipped the case and turned his attention to the portable file box. "Come on. It's blown whatever juice he had, but it'll recharge and come back. I can't stay with you and you sure as hell aren't staying alone."

"I already paid for the room," she said, rather stupidly, but this was moving too fast. She needed time to think.

"Damn it, Desi!" He loomed over her, his face set and hard. His dark eyes brooked no argument. "If I have to, I'll have you arrested for domestic violence. I mean it. I'll go to jail myself if that's what it takes."

She gasped. He did mean it. Gone was Buck the lover; here was Officer Walker ready to protect and serve—whether she wanted it or not.

Logical debate points failed to materialize in her brain. She couldn't even muster the desire to argue. He was right. No matter how unfair or unjust it was, no matter how angry or self-righteous she felt, Charles Skillihorn was going to keep coming until he got what he wanted. Trembling began in her knees and climbed through her body. She had to hug herself to keep from shaking.

He reached for her, but pulled back before touching her. Anguish twisted his brow. "I'll shoot myself before letting it use me to hurt you."

"Don't say that!"

He threw up his hands, looking as if he wanted something to grab, to rip apart. "I don't know what to do! Don't you understand that? I've run into this kind of evil before. They don't stop. They have an *eternity* to get what they want."

"So this is it? You leave me and I wait for Skillihorn to find another way to kill me? This is my life?"

"No!"

His pain was so open, so vulnerable, it took every ounce of Desi's strength to not rush into his arms to comfort and take comfort.

"I ran away from a Dark Presence before. It was bad, really bad. People died."

"It's not your fault," she whispered. "It can't be."

"It doesn't matter! I knew what was happening.

I could see it happening. I didn't know what to do. This time I will figure it out. This time I'm stopping it." He paced a tight circle, his hands opening and closing while he dragged in deep breaths. He tore back the draperies and scowled at the storm. "Damn it. I can't even take some personal time off of work. Right now you're going to your sister's or a friend's place. Or an all-night grocery store for all I care. You cannot be alone."

She nodded. "I'll go to Gwen's."

"I might have to pull extra shifts because of the storm. Give me Gwen's number. I'll contact you through her. When the storm lets up we'll get to the cemetery and see if Grandma shows up. I think she knows how to help. We just have to be smart enough to figure it out. Now get dressed and pack your stuff. I'll follow your car until you get where you need to go."

Even as a child she'd resisted being told what to do, hated being ordered around or prevented from doing things her way. Now, though, for the first time ever, she was more than happy to let someone else be in charge.

"OH, SWEETIE, what is wrong?" Gwen opened her arms and Desi walked into them. She rested her forehead against Gwen's shoulder. She was as close to crying as she'd ever been. Snow pelted her head and wind battered her back. It howled against the old brick building and made the metal staircase landing sway. Gwen grabbed Desi's suitcase and urged her inside, out of the storm.

Desi looked at the private parking lot behind the building. It had been a harrowing hour-long drive from the motel to here, creeping through snowdrifts while the wind tried to push her off the road and snow clotted on the windshield wipers, making it nearly impossible to see. Behind the building where Gwen lived Buck had driven into the alley first, breaking a trail with the Jeep's big tires so she could follow in her smaller vehicle. Now Buck flashed his headlights and eased away down the alley.

She swallowed the lump in her throat and entered her sister's apartment. Her shoulders ached from the tension of driving through the storm. Her stomach was so upset she feared she might throw up. She shoved the door closed against the wind and rested her head against the wood. Melting snow trickled down her face and the back of her neck.

"What happened?" Gwen clucked around Desi, helping her out of her wet coat and hat, and struggling to get Desi's boots off her feet. "You look terrible."

Desi managed a wan smile. "Thanks a lot." She followed her sister into the bedroom. Like the rest of the apartment and the antique store below it was cluttered and overdone, a kaleidoscope of colors and textures. It was like being back in Grandma's house. A sense of safety washed over Desi, a feeling of being grounded and almost back in control.

Spike hopped onto the bed and stomped over the

mounds of soft blankets and the quilted velvet and silk duvet. He made squeaky noises and purred as Desi hugged him.

Sighing and shaking her head, Gwen ordered Desi to change out of her wet clothing. Desi changed into her pajamas and wrapped an afghan around her shoulders against the chill. She sat on the bed and snuggled the cat until he had enough and struggled for her put him down. When Gwen returned with a steaming mug, Desi smelled alcohol. She looked up in question.

"Hot cocoa with a little extra." Gwen shrugged. "You look like you need it. Now tell me what's going on."

This was so strange. Desi felt as if she were outside herself, as if she watched from the sidelines. She was the strong one. She'd always taken care of Gwen. After their parents died she'd held her sister through the sad, endless nights and made sure she ate and washed and brushed her hair. After Grandma died, Desi had taken care of Gwen again, shielding her from having to deal with probating the estate and cleaning out Grandma's house to ready it for sale. Now she felt helpless and lost, unable to untangle her thoughts or see a course of action.

"Is it Buck?" Gwen asked her. "Did you guys have a fight?"

Aching for him tore her apart. Desi sighed. "I can't talk about it right now. I just can't. Can we talk in the morning?"

Gwen sat beside her and smoothed hair off Desi's forehead. "Tomorrow? When you're back to your old bossy self and I'm just a dumb kid too fragile for bad news? That tomorrow?"

Desi cringed.

"Why don't you let me take care of you for once? Honest to God, I'm not as stupid as you think I am."

Their earlier argument had been merely delayed, not finished. Weariness weighted Desi. Even the effort it took to hold the cup of cocoa seemed like too much. "All right, you want to help me. Then help." She looked around the bedroom with its frills and froufrou. The shadows looked normal. That, she knew, could change in a heartbeat. "Let me sleep in here, with you. With the light on. If you hear me doing anything weird in my sleep, even talking or snoring too loud, you wake me up. Dump a bucket of water on me if you have to. Just wake me up."

DESI FLIPPED A RECEIPT over and keyed in the figures from the next receipt into the spreadsheet. She still couldn't believe she'd slept. With Gwen snuggled against her back, as if they were kids again, and Spike pinning her feet, Desi had not only fallen asleep, she'd stayed asleep, a deep and dreamless sleep. She'd awakened alone in the bed. Gwen had been up for hours, and the store was open for business.

Desi felt rested, repaired and utterly miserable.

Desi had helped Gwen shovel and sweep snow from the sidewalk in front of the store. The storm had passed, leaving behind a brilliant blue sky and a brilliant white landscape. The entire city was blanketed and the road crews were out in full force, beginning with the main arteries and working their way through other streets. The busiest streets would be cleared first. Neighborhoods and back roads would have to wait. The sisters shoved snow around in the back parking lot, where snowdrifts reached up to eight feet against the building. They uncovered their cars. Not a trace of Desi's or Buck's passage remained from the night before. Gwen assured Desi that before too long one of her neighbors with a snowblower would clear the alley and give them access to the street. By the time they finished both had shed their coats and hats, and were so hot and sweaty that walking indoors felt like entering a sauna.

Bolstered with Gwen's excellent coffee Desi flew through her work with an energy she hadn't felt in ages.

She yearned for Buck. She wanted him to hold her. She wanted to finish what she'd started before the ghostly attack. She wanted to know he was okay.

Gwen entered the back room. She had a funny look on her face as she waved a scrap of paper. "I just got the strangest phone call."

Desi's heart skipped. *Please don't let Skillihorn start calling here.* As soon as she thought it, she knew it was silly. The ghost blew up phones. He didn't talk on them.

"Strange how?"

Gwen held up a finger indicating Desi should wait. She wiggled her shoulders, planted her feet and cleared her throat as though she were about to present Hamlet's soliloquy on stage. She read from the paper. 'All well here. Hope same for you. M. H. says go. Miss you.' She handed the paper to Desi. "Word for word, just like I was told. Who's M. H.?"

Desi's heart skipped another beat, this time in longing and fear of the coming confrontation. M. H. stood for Mary Hollyhock. *Grandma says go.* That could only mean the cemetery, which could only mean that Grandma had appeared to Buck. Desi felt relieved. Grandma disappeared when Skillihorn was around, so that meant Buck was safe. No worries about the ghost grabbing Buck and forcing him to crash his car into a gasoline tanker.

With a jingle of jewelry, Gwen pushed back her hair. "If you think I've forgotten we're supposed to talk, you're wrong." She pulled up a chair and sat, facing Desi. "Now what's going on?"

"Tell me who called with this."

"Will. He was very mysterious. He said I had to write the message word for word and give it to you. He also said the police are pulling extra shifts, so everyone is working overtime. I'm supposed to call him if you have any messages."

Resentment burned over a ghost forcing her to

play a juvenile game of Telephone. She really resented that Buck had evolved into He-Who-Shall-Not-Be-Named. The only thing preventing her from going into a rant was the cryptic "Miss you" on the note. Unless Gwen the hopeless romantic had added it just to stir the pot.

Buck would be so easy to fall in love with; she wasn't certain she was. Desirable, yes; sexy, apparently; but lovable? There her confidence died.

"How is Will?" Desi asked. "Have you gone out with him?"

"You're trying to distract me. Won't work."

"Have you?"

"Actually Will and Amber have a thing going. It's looking pretty serious, too. Now talk."

Desi balked. Who knew how long it would be before Alec could come down from Wyoming. She had no idea what was involved in "cleansing" and "purifying," or how long it would take. Even if Buck stayed away from her there was no way she could return to a motel or sleep by herself. The mere idea of awakening to find the ghost on top of her without even a cat to break its killer hold gave her a bad case of the willies. Gwen needed to know. Desi needed to know how Gwen would react if she did know. If Gwen resumed her insane obsession with the paranormal, Desi would never forgive herself.

Desi asked, "Did you dream about Grandma again?"

Gwen leaned back. She toyed with the chains

and beads around her neck. "You said dreams are neurotic brains."

"It's neurons firing in the brain," she corrected. "Now did you see Grandma?"

"Maybe."

"What did she say?"

Gwen wagged an admonishing finger. "You aren't that smart, girlie. I'm not giving you the chance to start making fun of me. You just want to change the subject."

"What did she say, Gwen, please?"

"'Trust me.' That's what she said. 'Trust me.'" Gwen frowned and her eyes narrowed in suspicion. "Do you have a head injury you're not telling me about? I'm the wackadoo in this family, not you."

Desi couldn't do it. Couldn't take the chance. She said, "I have a stalker."

Gwen gasped.

"See! This is why I don't want to tell you. Now you're scared."

"I'm not scared. I'm horrified. What has he done? Who is he?"

Desi didn't have to fib too much. "A guy named Charles, we think, but we're not certain. He's been in my house. He follows me. He wants to hurt—" She stopped before saying Buck's name, unwilling to disturb what little psychic peace she'd found. "—anyone I'm dating."

"Why didn't you tell me?"

"Because now you're all upset. I didn't take it

seriously at first. Now the police are handling it. I have to lie low for a few days."

Gwen pointed her chin at the mysterious message. "He hacked into your phone?"

"I guess. It seems that way. Can't take chances." Desi swiveled the chair. The back of her neck burned. She was good at concealing the truth, but telling an outright lie made her stomach quiver. The very air surrounding her felt thick with disapproval. "The police are handling it. I'm safe for now."

"Should I close the store? Lock the door and set the alarm?"

"Don't do that. I'm fine, really. Um, the cops are setting up a sting operation. They'll catch him. Everything will be okay." A nudge on the shoulder startled her. She whipped her head about.

"Do you hear something?" Gwen whispered, her eyes round and fearful.

Desi touched the spot where she'd been touched. *Empty your head,* she thought frantically. No thinking, no fear to give him power. Nobody had touched her. She was safe here.

"I'm just jumpy. It's okay." She faced the computer. "I'm so sorry to get you involved in this. I'm nervous enough for both of us. I hate upsetting you."

Gwen stood and flung back her glorious head. "I am not upset! I am royally pissed off. Nobody messes with the Hollyhock girls and gets away with it."

Desi snickered, suddenly loving her sister more than ever.

"Don't laugh at me." Gwen karate-chopped the air. "I have a few dirty tricks up my sleeve." She waggled a foot toward Desi. Her boots had three-inch heels. "See these stilettos? Lethal."

"Lethal to you if you fall off of them." Her giggle turned into a laugh. "Thank you, Gwen. I mean that. Thanks for making me talk."

"Do you have a message to send?"

I miss you so much my insides are crumbling. And I really, really, really want to see you naked! That's what she wanted to say. Instead, she said, "Yeah." She printed on a sticky note, "All okay here. Name time and place." She handed it to Gwen, who wrinkled her nose.

"This is for Buck? Nothing else?"

"That's it. Call Will and ask him to pass it on." Gwen left the back room, and Desi's bad feelings returned. She should not have lied. Gwen was a grown-up, a business owner, and no longer a broken-hearted girl with too much money and a burning obsession to find her lost loves.

A clatter startled her. She snapped her attention to a narrow shelf mounted on the wall above the desk. It was covered with old perfume bottles of various shapes and sizes. Desi stood and noticed a picture frame facedown on the shelf. She picked it up. It was a photo of her grandmother wearing a snowsuit, her blonde hair blowing in the wind. Desi remembered taking this photo during a ski trip in Breckenridge.

"Grandma?" she whispered. "Is that you? Did you touch me?" She turned a slow circle, looking up and down and in every corner. She set the photograph back on the shelf.

Five minutes later Gwen breezed back in with a slip of paper. Buck's reply said: "Really?"

"This is it? Really what?"

Gwen caught her lower lip in her teeth and raised her eyes to the ceiling. "Well…"

"What did you do?" Desi rose, glaring at her sister. "Gwendolyn."

"Your message was so blah. I just, you know—" she lifted a shoulder "—told him how you feel."

"How I feel? Gwen! What did you say to him?"

"I didn't say anything. *You* said it. I just told him you loved him." Gwen scooted out of the back room, leaving Desi with her mouth hanging open and wondering if Buck's "Really?" was a good thing or a bad thing.

She stomped to the door and yelled, "When this is all over, Gwen, I'm going to kill you!"

Gwen's laughter filled the store. "Trust me, sweetie. You'll thank me."

DESPITE THE WEATHER, or because of it, Hollyhock Antiques and Oddities enjoyed brisk business. From the back room Desi listened to would-be buyers haggling with Gwen. People had braved the icy, slushy, slippery streets in the hopes of beating out people who refused to venture outside. To Desi it seemed Gwen was off her game. She let a few good offers slip through her hands, and she sold some items for far less than they were worth. Gwen wasn't flirting outrageously, either. Desi felt badly about it, knowing it was her fault.

She'd backed herself into a tight corner with the lame story about a stalker. Either she'd have to keep her imaginary stalker hanging around the rest of her life or eventually try to explain the lack of details about his arrest, trial and imprisonment. Whenever she worked up the nerve to tell Gwen the truth, her imagination filled with what-ifs. What if Gwen started holding séances again? What if she trapped Grandma on this plane of existence? What if she tried to contact their parents or her fiancé? What if she hooked up with a phony medium and lost what little money she had left? What if she pestered Buck about ghosts, calling him day and night, until Buck forgot all about Desi and fell in love with Gwen?

Desi threw herself into her work. She caught up all the previous month's bookkeeping, e-mailed end-of-year reports and spent hours on the phone, double-checking figures with clients and their CPAs. She even paid her bills and balanced her checking accounts.

Numbers, always faithful numbers, saved her from worrying about what Skillihorn's next nasty trick might be.

Gwen popped into the back room. "Guess what? I sold both those barrister bookcases! The Fell & Rogers. Full price."

Desi breathed, "Wow."

"Now who's the queen of the deal?" Giggling, she returned to the front of the store.

Desi remembered her head nearly exploding when Gwen dropped two grand apiece for the mahogany bookcases, at a time when Gwen had barely two hundred bucks in the store's business account. They'd been on display close to six months, with $5,200 price tags on each one, and Desi figured Gwen would still own them when she was a little old lady.

A nudge on her shoulder almost made her scream. She swiveled the chair so fast she nearly lost her balance. "Stop it," she whispered, searching corners for any sign of a ghostly presence. Her heart hammered. "If that's you, Grandma, you have to stop. My nerves are shot."

Her phone trilled and she did jump. She spun around so fast she stumbled and had to grab a filing cabinet to keep from falling.

She picked up the phone, half expected to see "Afterlife" on the caller ID. It was her neighbor, Annaliese.

She forced a bright tone. "Well, hi, Annaliese, how are you?"

"The question is, how are you? I have not seen you in many days and you did not clear the snow from your walk. I knocked on your door and rang the bell. You are not home. Never home now. I worry you are sick or in hospital."

"No, no, I'm fine," Desi said. She should have known her uncleared porch and walk would alarm Annaliese. The woman tolerated no snowflakes, fallen leaves or blown dirt on her walkway. Her tiny front yard and window boxes were always pristine. Her front door and windows always sparkled. If Desi slacked, Annaliese looked askance. "Just taking a little vacation. I'm sorry I didn't tell you. I didn't mean to worry you."

"That is a relief." She chuckled. "A vacation with that handsome man? He is what you girls call a hottie, right?"

Desi grinned. "Yes, ma'am." She bit her lower lip to keep from asking Annaliese to check her house. She didn't want her neighbor to catch Skillihorn napping on her bed, or something worse.

"You be careful," Annaliese said. "Sometimes a man is too handsome, you know? My Jeffrey was too handsome and look what happened to me!"

Desi laughed. Annaliese's handsome husband had taken her all over the world, given her four children and a lifetime of memories.

"When will you be home? Would you like me to use my key and make sure all is right inside? I should check the pipes for freezing."

The question offered some comfort. If Skillihorn were tearing up the house or turning the television or radio off and on, Annaliese would know. "That's okay. I'll be home in a few days."

She hoped.

Chapter Thirteen

Buck entered his apartment. Thirty hours on shift and he was so tired he couldn't feel his legs and feet. He dropped his coat on the couch and arched his back until his spine popped. His eyes burned with fatigue and he yawned for the fifth time in a row.

Snow patrol was a bitch. It meant hours spent guarding downed power lines until the utilities trucks could make it to the scene; untangling the stories of motorists who had ice-skated their vehicles through intersections only to collide with other vehicles doing the same thing. Then there were the disputes between neighbors about snow removal; business break-ins by homeless men hoping to be arrested so they could wait out the storm in the jail; frantic calls by people worried about elderly shut-ins. He'd caught a few catnaps at the station, but mostly he'd just consumed far too much coffee.

Moving on autopilot, he unbuckled his service belt and placed his sidearm, pepper spray and Taser in the gun safe. When he removed his Kevlar vest, his skin seemed to breathe a sigh of relief. His uniform went in a pile to be dealt with later.

He flopped facedown on the couch to rest for a minute.

He dreamed of Desi. She waited for him on a warm beach while he swam through the ocean toward her. He had come a long, long way and she was the prize awaiting him. Every stroke of his arms through the surf made him feel stronger. Every breath filled him with power. She stood on the blinding white sand, her dark hair impossibly long and blowing sinuously in a tropical breeze. She waved at him. "I'm coming," he yelled. "Wait for me!" Her waving turned frantic and she began to scream. He floated on the now-still waters. A dark shadow passed below him, dark and menacing and immense, gliding like a slow torpedo toward Desi. He tried to yell at her to run, but the sea grabbed at him, filling his mouth and throat with bitter salt, dragging him under, pulling him back...

Buck startled awake, gasping and disoriented.

He struggled to his feet, his muscles protesting. He checked his wristwatch and stared at it in disbelief. Four hours had passed since he walked in the door.

A muffled roar drew him to the window. The apartment complex maintenance guys were in the parking lot, clearing snow with a plow mounted on a lawn tractor. Bared asphalt steamed. The brilliant sun washed color from the world. Snowdrifts, built higher by the passage of snowplows, blocked his view of the street.

Desi. His nerve endings burned with his desire to see her. Talk to her. Hold her. The nightmare had drained from him, but dread remained.

He wandered into the bathroom, stripped, then started the shower. While the water heated, he examined his scruffy face in the mirror. He had a dark bruise on his chin from Desi kicking him, but it was more colorful than painful. What still hurt was the bump on his head. He gingerly touched his head, relieved the swelling had disappeared. Some kind of girl-law, he supposed: the smaller the woman, the bigger the purse.

No matter how busy he'd been during the storm, he couldn't stop thinking about Desi. He couldn't stop thinking about her message. *All okay here. Name time and place. I love you.*

I love you.

He sighed. Like the jackass he was, he'd asked Will to ask her, *Really?*

Really?

Like a teenager passing notes in algebra class. Like an idiot who didn't know a good thing when he held it in his hands.

He'd dated plenty of women, but the *knowing* did him in every time. Knowing their little lies, knowing their games, always knowing how they truly felt. Too much *knowing.*

The more he knew Desi the more he wanted to

know. Her temper, her confidence, her independence, the way she talked so tough, and yet her
heart was so tender. Stirrings of arousal made him
grin. It didn't hurt that she was the sexiest woman
he'd ever met.

Did he love her?

Did he want to?

He did.

He should have called her right away. It hurt to
know she was only a phone call away, but he
couldn't contact her. It hurt knowing she was only
a few miles away, but he couldn't see her face.

"Idiot," he growled at his reflection. He should
have told Will to tell Desi *I love you, too.*

Mary Hollyhock's face appeared in the mirror.
Startled, he grabbed a washcloth to cover his groin
and spun about. Her image disappeared.

"Not funny," he said. "Do you mind?"

The shower was beginning to steam. He stepped
into the tub and closed the curtain as if that could
hide his nakedness from a ghost. "We'll talk when
I finish," he said. He lifted his face to the pulse of
hot water, letting it burn off the fatigue. The smile
he'd glimpsed on Mary's lovely face in the mirror
reassured him Desi was safe. The dread lifted.

He shampooed his hair. It felt as if a third hand
worked its way through his hair and against his
scalp. He slapped at the phantom hand. "Ma'am!
Please. I can wash myself." After he rinsed his hair,
he hesitated about picking up the soap and wash-

cloth. He did *not* want Desi's grandmother—anybody's grandmother!—washing his ass.

To his relief she left him alone while he finished, then stepped out, dried off and pulled on a pair of shorts. He decided not to shave. He was too hungry.

In the kitchen he checked his cell phone. No missed calls. He wanted to hear Desi's voice and assure himself that she really was safe, but he didn't dare. Their connection attracted the Dark Presence, and he could not risk it. He pulled eggs from the fridge.

He glimpsed a flash of rhinestones from the corner of his eye. She was here, but her manifestation was weak. "Are you afraid of drawing him to me?" She materialized enough for him to see her nod. "He can't enter the cemetery. So we can talk there, right?" She nodded again. He could see the clock on the wall through her filmy image. "Do you know how to get rid of him? What he wants?" Another nod.

The apartment felt empty and he knew he was alone. Still, fear coiled in his belly like a cold, heavy snake. He felt ten years old again, terrified but fascinated by his first encounter with a Dark Presence. He blinked rapidly, trying not to go there, but he remembered its black emptiness and the way it looked at him. It had no eyes, but a stare like tentacles, drawing him in. His arms ached with the memory of powerful, invisible hands making him reach for a box of kitchen matches stinking of sulfur. His shoulders ached with memories of struggling against it only to have it push him, drag him, yank him out the door and across the fields. His mouth moved and his lungs breathed, but another voice sang *Make it burn. Make it burn.* Tears streamed down his cheeks as corn leaves sliced his skin.

He shook himself and slammed both fists against the counter. Genuine pain rocketed through his arms and broke the memories. He shook his head so hard that his tears struck the kitchen cabinet.

His mouth filled with sour despair.

He snatched up the phone to call Will. This had to end. Somehow, someway, it had to end.

BUCK SPOTTED DESI'S CAR in the cemetery. The bright-red Subaru stood out against fields of snow. He drove slowly along the plowed and dry road wending through the cemetery. Deep snow covered the fields in a lumpy blanket, shrouding headstones and shrubs. Spruce and fir trees were white sentinels, their branches weighted.

He parked behind the Subaru, then sat for a moment, his mind open and searching. He felt certain he'd understood Mary Hollyhock that the Dark Presence had no power here, but the fear snake stirred in his belly.

He got out of the Jeep.

I love you.

What would a man do to be worthy of her love?

Die for her. For her love he'd go the other side and battle Charles Skillihorn ghost to ghost.

Desi stepped out of the car. The sight of her nearly took him to his knees. Her hair flowed like dark water, gleaming beneath the sun. Dark sunglasses shielded her eyes. A forest-green sweater clung to her slender curves.

She looked uncertain as she stood with her hand atop the open car door. "Hi."

He stood his ground, cursing the twenty feet that separated them. He blinked against the bright snow glittering like diamonds and slipped on his sunglasses. "Crazy how warm it is, eh?"

She nodded. "That's the nice thing about late-season storms." She suddenly slammed the car door. "Are we nuts, Buck? Standing in a cemetery talking about the weather?"

She shoved the keys in her pocket and marched toward him with a fierceness that momentarily stunned him. It turned him on, too. When she grasped his hands with a surprisingly strong grip he swayed with dizziness.

Her throat worked with a hard swallow. He could see her eyes behind the glasses, searching, demanding. "Did you…? What you said. Do you mean it?"

The last message he'd sent through Will via Gwen had been to the point. *Cemetery. Today. 2:00.* Since she was here he was here and she knew he meant it.

Unless she meant his idiot reply to her "I love you." *Really?*

He was so far out of his realm he didn't know

whether to laugh, run like hell or drop to his knees and beg forgiveness for what had to have seemed like a dismissal. He shook his head. Or maybe it was what he didn't say. After he relayed the message to Will, he knew he should have told Desi he loved her. It was difficult enough to express how he felt without having to do it through emissaries.

"I'm sorry. It was stupid. I didn't mean to sound like that."

She dropped her hands. "Oh."

Her sudden coldness and the hurt in her eyes meant he'd said the wrong thing, the worst thing.

"I'm gonna kill Gwen. That liar," she muttered. She turned away and shoved her hands in her pockets. "Are we alone?"

Uncertain what Desi's sister had to do with this, but certain he was in trouble, he said, "Honey, please, come on. Don't be made at me."

She turned her head enough to see him. "I'm not mad."

"Have a heart. This is new to me. I mean, a girl like you. A woman like you! You're so—"

She spun about. "I'm so what? Mean? Bad-tempered? Snotty? Short?"

Somehow, some way, their trains of thought had diverged and they weren't talking about the same thing at all. He trod dangerous ground filled with land mines that could blow his heart to pieces. "You're so incredible," he said quietly. He pulled off his sunglasses and squinted against the glare.

She slid her sunglasses atop her head and peered suspiciously at his face. "Then it was you? You mean it."

He nodded. He didn't trust his stupid mouth. His stupid brain couldn't come up with anything better than *incredible* to describe her. He stretched a hand toward her and waited. She placed her delicate hand in his. He drew her close and kissed her. Her lips were cold, hesitant, but they quickly warmed, and her eagerness swept him away from the snow-shrouded graves. Away from fear and confusion. Her sweet lips parted and her tongue was hot silk. He held her closer, aching to take her to that huge bed of hers. He wanted her naked and hot and making those wanton noises that drove him wild. He wanted to show her with his mouth and his hands and his body how incredible and beautiful and lovable she was.

She pushed his shoulder and broke the kiss. Her mouth was red, her eyes dark. She searched his face. "Are we alone?" she whispered.

Blinded by arousal, he blinked in order to focus. His head cleared. He saw no Dark Presence. No grandmother, either. "Yeah."

"What are we supposed to do?"

All kinds of ideas popped into his head, and none involved appropriate behavior. He shifted his hips, trying to readjust his jeans, and wondered if throwing himself face-first into the snow would help cool his blood. He forced himself to turn her loose.

"We don't have to go to the grave, do we?" She eyed the snow. They'd parked as closely to the Skillihorn graves as possible but reaching those graves still meant a hike through wet snow over hilly, uneven ground.

"Call your grandmother."

She hugged herself and shivered. Buck felt the cold then. As bright as the sun was, it was fool's-gold warmth. Intermittent wind lifted a chill off the snow and sent it coursing around his body.

"Let's sit in your car, honey. Warm up a bit."

Once they were inside the Subaru, she turned on the engine so the heater blew over their feet.

"Call her," Buck said.

Desi loosed a long breath. "Grandma?" Her cheeks reddened and she placed both hands over her mouth. A nervous giggle escaped through her fingers.

Astonished, Buck said, "You still don't believe."

"I do! I've seen him. Heard him." She touched her throat. "Felt him. I do believe."

Buck shook his head. "You're still trying to explain this away. Still looking for loopholes."

He sensed her presence before he saw her. Mary Hollyhock appeared in the backseat, as solid as flesh and blood. She wore a soft sweater and cream-colored slacks. A triple row of pearls encircled her neck and big clusters of pearls decorated her ears. A brooch with pearls and rhinestones glittered on the sweater. Her hands were folded primly on her lap. A smirk gave away her ladylike ruse of pretending she hadn't been pestering him while he showered.

Desi shifted on the seat to follow his gaze. "Why are you smiling?"

"Your grandmother has quite a sense of humor."

Desi craned her neck, trying to see the floor behind her. "Is she here?"

"Yep. So, ma'am, what do we do?"

He heard it deep within his mind. Heard it in his heart. *Forgive.*

"Forgive," he said, and the spirit nodded in reply.

"Forgive what?" Desi asked.

Buck sighed. For all she'd seen, for all she'd felt, she still hadn't taken that final leap of faith. Still couldn't accept that there existed a world beyond her senses, a world beyond the reach of science.

"I don't think Desi believes you're here."

Mary laughed silently. On her neat lap appeared a plate of cookies. Buck frowned at them. They looked like the macaroons he'd bought for Desi, but these were speckled with something dark. He caught a whiff of… He sniffed, trying to catch the elusive scent. Chocolate.

"I do believe," Desi insisted. "I just don't know what she means!"

"Macaroons with chocolate?" He stared at the cookies. "Chocolate chips?"

Desi fell back against the door, staring at him with wide eyes. She whispered, "What did you say?"

"She's showing me cookies. Coconut macaroon

cookies with chocolate chips in them." He inhaled deeply, but the scent was gone. "It smelled good for a moment. I—"

Tears filled Desi's eyes. Her chin quivered and her lips parted.

"Honey? Desi?"

One tear spilled, then another. She wailed and dropped her face in her hands. Her shoulders shook.

Buck reached for her, but she twisted away, as much as the narrow seat and steering wheel allowed. The console frustrated Buck's efforts to gather her in his arms.

He resorted to patting her back. "Honey, don't cry. Please don't cry."

She lifted her face to him. It was red and wet. "I'm not crying! I never cry!" she protested. Then she resumed sobbing.

Buck looked to Mary for help. She gazed serenely out the window at the snow falling in clumps from evergreen limbs.

This had happened many times before. A spirit would show him something personal and it struck a chord with the disbeliever, loosing a deluge of emotion. Buck hated it. It made him feel mean-spirited, as if he made people cry for the hell of it. The spirits were never any help. They always acted as if this was exactly the reaction they wanted.

"I bet you liked soap operas," Buck muttered to her.

Mary lifted an elegant eyebrow.

Desi's sobbing eased and the snuffling began.

She got a package of tissues out of the console and blew her nose. Ripped out a fresh tissue and wiped her face. Another tissue, another nose blow. She continued blowing and wiping her face until the tissue pack was empty.

"I'm glad you never cry, honey. That could get messy."

She shot him a glare through swollen eyes and pulled down the visor to look in the mirror. She groaned.

"Why can't I see her, Buck?" Her voice was rough and her shoulders hitched. "It's not fair that you can see her and I can't. Does she look good? Is she happy?"

"She's beautiful."

Mary preened, touching her hair and lifting her chin to show off the elegant length of her neck.

Desi twisted and reached between the seats for her purse. She pulled it onto her lap and began rummaging. "Where is she? Where exactly? What is she doing?"

"She's sitting in the back seat. Behind you."

She searched the mirror for a sign of anything behind her. "Is that what this is all about, Grandma? You brought me here because of those damned cookies? You want forgiveness? Fine, you're forgiven."

Curious, though not surprised by the roller coaster of her emotions, he looked between Desi and her grandmother. The spirit was beginning to look pale. Sunlight turned her hair into a shimmering corona lacking true form. She was losing power.

"Talk to her, Desi," he said. "About whatever you need to say. I don't think she can stay here much longer."

"Talk about what? Macaroons?" She smiled. It was weak and her eyes were strained. "Grandma made the best macaroons in the whole world." She spoke into the mirror. "You did. I've never had better. They were my special treat. She made them just for me." She rummaged in the purse and found a fresh pack of tissues. She blew her nose again. "When I got my first acceptance letter for college she made extra-special macaroons." She twisted on the seat, doing her best to see behind her. "She screwed them up royally with chocolate chips!"

Mary shrugged and showed her palms. Her rhinestone brooch had lost its glitter. Buck could see the door seam and seat belt through her.

Desi slumped. "I pitched a fit." She covered her eyes with a hand. "Like a two-year-old. I accused her of trying to ruin my great news. Oh God, I was horrid. I acted like a brat." She dabbed at her eyes. "A horrible, spoiled brat. Selfish and ungrateful and mean! I'm sorry, Grandma! I am so, so sorry. I miss you so much."

Now the spirit was little more than a shadow.

A gentle voice only Buck could hear said, "Forgive."

Her power flared, filling the car interior with

light. Her face was suddenly young, unlined. Her face belonged to Gwen.

She disappeared.

Beside him, Desi explained, "I was so stressed out. I applied to about six colleges and I was totally convinced all of them would reject me. Chocolate chips shouldn't have set me off, but maybe it was just too much. It's embarrassing just to think about it."

"She's gone, honey."

She twisted and grasped the headrest, searching. "Gone? Are you sure?"

"I'm sure."

She slumped, her chin nearly to her chest. "You would have hated me in high school. I was such a snot. I never did tell her I was sorry. Too self-righteous. Can she hear me? I'm sorry, Grandma. I really am. I love you." She looked in the mirror and groaned. "Don't look at me, Buck. I'm a mess." She brought out a comb and began swiping at her hair with the jerky motions of an agitated cat.

A stirring in his groin surprised him. Who knew feminine vanity turned him on? It took some mental tugging to bring his thoughts back to the problem at hand. Forgiveness was the key to stopping the Dark Presence. It had to be.

He watched her grooming, amazed by the number of products she hauled around in that lethal purse. Lotions, potions and powder to smooth, daub and brush over her face with deft, practiced fingers and a prodigious number of different-sized and textured applicators.

He rubbed a hand over his jaw. Shaving was nothing compared to this.

"Gwen is part of this," he said.

"Why?" Her face was smooth and pale again but her eyes were still swollen. "She's got nothing to do with Skillihorn."

He turned his gaze to the snowfields, looking for Veronica's grave. The trees seemed to steam as they dropped loads of snow. The answer danced just outside his reach.

Inside himself, he felt consumed by the need to talk, to unburden his own soul the way Desi had. "I saw a Dark Presence when I was ten," he said in a low voice. "The first I'd ever seen. It scared me, but it was fascinating, too. The way climbing tall trees or hornet nests are fascinating. You know they're dangerous, but you can't stay away." He shrugged. "At least, it's that way for ten-year-old boys. I made it notice me."

"What happened?"

"It tried to make me burn down a house."

"Why?"

"I don't know. I still don't know. It was a meth lab. The meth-heads had a bunch of kids. They were always dirty, hungry. I figure some really nasty things happened in that house."

"Did you? Burn down the house?"

He shook his head. "It forced me through the

cornfields, up to the house. I had matches. Then I stepped in a hole and busted my face. It disappeared and I ran. After that when I felt it I'd slap my hands over my ears and sing, really loud. I'd pinch and punch myself." He chuckled. "No wonder people thought I was weird."

"So you beat it," Desi said.

The momentary amusement faded. "The meth lab blew up and the house burned down. Four people died, including one of the kids."

He could see her processing the story. She was smart. She'd figure out on her own that Dark Presences got what they wanted, one way or another.

"I stopped contacting spirits after that. Refused to acknowledge them. Refused to give them any indication I could see them. After a while they were like background noise. I almost made myself believe they weren't real."

"What happened? What made you start communicating again?" She rubbed his arm.

He cursed the compact car. He wanted to hold her, though whether to give comfort or take it he wasn't certain. "A girl in my freshman English class at Nebraska State. Her brother's spirit needed to stop her from committing suicide. He'd committed suicide and needed to stop hers. After that, as long as I was really careful, I could help people."

Forgive, he mused, turning it over in his mind. He snapped his head about and stared at the graves. "Veronica. We have to summon Veronica."

Desi's mouth dropped open. "No! You saw what he did to her. He cut off her head, Buck! We can't force her to face him again. You said yourself that spirits are afraid of Dark Presences. What if he sucks her into whatever hell he's created for himself?"

Guilt crept through his chest and up his throat. He couldn't meet Desi's eyes. "She's the only one who can forgive him."

"She's had over a hundred years to forgive him. Was she at the Moore house? Did you sense her presence there at all?"

He shook his head.

"Then she's at peace. She's over on the other side doing whatever it is that spirits do. We can't drag her back. It's cruel."

"You grandmother—"

"Maybe she's wrong! She wasn't perfect when she was alive. She's not perfect now." Desi looked around. "I'm sorry, Grandma, but the truth is the truth."

He slumped on the seat, waiting for the *knowing*. It didn't come. "We'll talk to Alec." He looked at her, studied her beautiful face, unable to bear the idea of never being able to hold her again, to show her how much he loved her. "Maybe she's talking about you."

"What do you mean?"

"Mary showed me Gwen. Maybe you need to forgive Gwen."

"For what? I love her."

"She needs to forgive you?"

Desi opened her mouth as if to protest, but the fight drained from her and her gaze turned distant and sad.

"How old were you when your parents died?"

Her eyes began looking watery again and he braced for a second flood. "I was six, Gwen was four, almost five."

"A car accident."

"It wasn't an accident. They were murdered by a drunk driver." She ripped a tissue from the pack and dabbed at her carefully made-up eyes. "Grandma died three years ago. It was so sudden. We never got to say goodbye."

"I think you're doing what Gwen does but in a different way. Gwen finds haunted objects and you stay pissed off. You're trying to convince yourself that dead is dead and that's all there is so maybe the losses won't hurt so much. Have you two ever talked about your losses? Really talked?"

"Well, sure! I mean…" She caught her lower lip in her teeth. She turned big, sad, red-rimmed eyes on him. "I guess we haven't. So what do we do? How will talking to Gwen make Skillihorn go away?"

He cupped her chin in his hand. She sighed and leaned into his touch. "There's a lot of power in for-giveness. Gwen must be the fourth for our circle. We combine our power, stand together and we can force Skillihorn to go away."

Chapter Fourteen

Here, Desi realized, was the real problem of a lifetime of skeptical thinking. Now that she was face-to-face with Gwen, and she needed desperately to enlist her sister's help, and her very life depended on trusting the wisdom of her dead grandmother, a huge part of her was going, *Huh? Are you nuts?*

Gwen sat behind the service counter sorting through a box of estate jewelry. The obvious junk and broken pieces went in one pile. Those she would sell online for arts and crafts. Designer pieces and antiques went in another. She pressed each and every piece, including broken plastic flowers, against her cheek and closed her eyes, seeking the vibes of residual ghosts.

Desi looked out the front door of the shop. The streetlights were on. Restaurants and bars lining Tejon street were lit up. In the shadow of Pikes Peak night came early to Colorado Springs. All day solar power had melted the snow, and the gutters now ran like rivers. The temperature was dropping, and any standing water would soon turn to ice. Cars cruised with the creep-and-freeze motion of cats on the prowl, seeking a wily parking spot.

"Do you have a date?" Gwen asked.

"What?"

"You've been staring out the door ever since I closed."

Alec was coming in tomorrow. Tomorrow they would send Skillihorn to hell.

Dallas agreed with Buck. Gwen had to be the fourth member of their circle. Desi wanted to throw up.

"Is he good in bed?"

"Gwen!"

"Oh come on. If he's clumsy or stupid, that's okay. You can train him. It's the selfish ones you need to dump. No hope for them." Gwen tapped her chin with a finger. "Nope, can't see Buck being selfish. He strikes me as the attentive type. Does he look as good naked as I imagine?"

"Gwendolyn!"

She flung back her head and her laughter filled the store. "I wish you could see your face! It's so red I bet it glows in the dark."

"My sex life is none of your business. And I don't appreciate you drooling over Buck like that." Desi drew her head aside. "Just how many men have you slept with anyway?"

"You'd be shocked by the number," Gwen said with a too-innocent smile.

"You can't count that high?"

"Ooh, claws." Gwen held up a huge, diamond-bright rhinestone brooch and peered through a loupe at the back of it. "I thought so. Eisenberg Sterling. This piece will pay for the entire lot. Very nice." She turned the brooch back and forth, catching the light and making it sparkle as if it were on fire. "One."

Desi scowled at the door, wishing time would hurry. She'd put off Skillihorn forever, if possible, but she ached to see Buck again. All the sex talk centered the ache in her pelvis and increased her anxiety. "One what?"

"One guy. I've slept with just one guy."

"Get outta here!"

"You think you know me so well, Desdemona." Gwen chuckled, rather evilly. "I love that look on your face."

"Who was it? Is it somebody you're seeing now?"

Gwen fussed with the box of jewelry, rattling pieces around as if the Hope diamond might be jumbled up in the tangle of old pearls and chains. She said, "Jesse."

A wave of sorrow washed through Desi. Major Jesse Vandell, Gwen's handsome soldier, the love of her life. They'd been engaged and Grandma had the wedding planned and Gwen had a wedding gown that rivaled Princess Di's and Desi had been fitted for a silk maid of honor's dress. Then two weeks before Jesse was supposed to come home from Iraq, his helicopter went down and he died.

Desi looked beyond her sister to the glass case

filled with jewelry and artifacts from the Middle East. A case she never opened for customers. Gwen was searching for her lost Jesse's soul.

"Well, shoot," Gwen said. She spoke lightly, but sorrow's darkness lurked in her eyes. "A bad reputation is a lot more fun than a goody-goody one."

Desi leaned her forearms on the service counter. "I'm sorry."

"About what?"

"For thinking I knew you so well. Can you forgive me?"

"Sure. As long as you give me all the juicy details about Buck."

Desi blushed again and ducked her head. "I think I'm in love with him."

Gwen flipped a hand. "That's old news. How is he in the sack?"

"Gwen!"

"Oh come on. Five minutes with the two of you and anyone can tell you're star-crossed lovers. Romeo and Juliet, Tristan and Isolde, Lancelot and Guineviere. Well, except for the tragedy part with everybody dying. But you know what I mean. You're meant for each other. As long he's not selfish in bed. That would be very disappointing."

"If you don't sleep around, how do you know this stuff?"

"I read *Cosmo*."

When it came to Buck Walker, *selfish* wasn't in the vocabulary. Desi sighed. Grandma said she and

Gwen had to forgive each other, and this conversation gave Desi a pretty good idea what needed forgiving. "There's something I have to show you."

"Ooh, this sounds ominous. Want to go grab some dinner?"

"Later." She suspected anything she ate right now would come right back up. She went to the back room and sat down at the computer. She pulled up Rampart's Web site and logged on. Gwen watched over her shoulder.

Desi pulled up the pages of Tara's research about the Moore house. She scrolled down to the crime-scene photographs.

"Eww," Gwen said. Never taking her eyes off the screen, she pulled up a chair and sat next to Desi. "Is that a body?"

"Her name was Veronica Skillihorn. This is from 1898. Her husband killed her, then framed the gardener. People called the gardener the Italian monster. They hanged him. Charles Skillihorn got away with two murders." She scrolled down to the gruesome photograph of Veronica's head. "He cut off her head." She hesitated, then blurted, "He's my stalker."

Gwen frowned at her.

"When we investigated the Moore house I did something really, really stupid. I invited the ghost to come home with me. Now he's trying to kill me."

"A ghost? You?" She looked between Desi and the computer screen.

Desi told her sister everything about the young ghost and the Dark Presence, the supernatural activity in her house, and being choked first by the ghost and then by Buck, and how it didn't matter if she stayed out of her house because Skillihorn showed up whenever Buck was around.

Desi kind of wished Gwen would scoff or laugh or even ask a question. Something about her credulity, though it didn't surprise her, did unnerve her.

"There's more," Desi said. "Buck is psychic. He can communicate with ghosts."

Now Gwen laughed.

"It's not funny."

"You said psychics are all fakes. Now the love of your life is psychic. That's kind of funny."

Desi crossed her arms, saying nothing.

"I'm sorry!" Gwen hurried to apologize. "How in the world did he convince you, of all people, that he's psychic?"

To Desi's horror her throat was tightening up and her eyes felt gritty. She didn't want to cry anymore. She turned her attention back to the screen and the photograph of Veronica Skillihorn. "He's been talking to Grandma."

"Grandma as in our grandma?"

Desi nodded.

"I knew it! I knew it was her hanging around. How is she?"

"Fine, I suppose." A new kind of jealousy rose.

Gwen didn't bother with cynicism or skepticism. Gwen had the capacity to believe. She could take on faith that which she didn't understand and never felt compelled to go to war with the universe in order to find the answers. "Buck is the real thing."

"I thought there was something kind of otherworldly about him."

"Grandma is helping us get rid of Skillihorn."

"That's Grandma, the warrior queen. Remember that guy in the parking lot? The one who left the cart in the handicapped space?"

Desi did remember. That man had looked seven feet tall and he'd had tattoos and an ugly expression, but Grandma had reamed him for his inconsideration. The man had not only taken his cart to the corral, he'd gathered a few others left by thoughtless shoppers. Desi giggled.

"Remember," Gwen said, "when that awful waiter spilled water on me and Grandma made him apologize?" She dissolved into giggles. "Remember how she corrected the grammar and spelling when the school sent letters home begging for votes to raise taxes?" She made a stern, disapproving face. "'My goodness, how can I expect you to properly educate our children when you insist on putting an apostrophe after its?'" Her imitation of Grandma was spot-on.

Desi and Gwen both laughed, and within minutes they were hanging onto each other, laughing like loons, until both were breathless.

When Desi finally got herself under control, she said, "Grandma says I'm supposed to forgive you. Or you're supposed to forgive me."

"Why?"

"She wasn't all that clear. Buck says it's about emotional power. Spirits can draw energy from negative emotions. Anything you want to get off your chest? Anything you need forgiveness for?"

Gwen waggled a hand toward the computer, indicating she wanted the gory picture gone. Desi minimized the screen. She turned her chair so she and Gwen sat knee to knee.

Finally Gwen said, "Can you forgive me for telling Ricky Morales you stuffed your bra?"

Puzzled, drawing a blank, Desi cocked her head. "I've been wearing a C cup since sixth grade. Why would I stuff my bra? And who's Ricky Morales?"

"Oh. Never mind." Gwen's cheeks turned pink.

"No! This is about everything between us. Who's Ricky?"

"Junior high. He thought you were cute. He wanted to be your boyfriend. You don't remember him? Really black hair. Kind of buck-toothed, but adorable?"

The blank refused to fill. "You told him I stuffed my bra?"

"If you don't even remember, what's the point of asking you to forgive me?"

Desi shook an admonishing finger. "You aren't getting off that easy. Why in the world would you say such a mean thing? I was really self-conscious about my boobs."

"Ricky liked you." Gwen toyed with the line of bracelets encircling her wrist. "He didn't like me. I guess I was jealous. I did a lot of mean things back in junior high and high school. You were always better than me."

"You were jealous of me?"

"You were perfect! Straight *A*s, advanced classes. The teachers loved you. And you were so confident! It was like you didn't need anybody. You never took crap from anybody. I agonized over people liking me, but you didn't care."

That wasn't the way Desi remembered high school at all. She'd felt like a freak, a misfit, a total nerd. "I thought *you* were the perfect one. Beautiful. A zillion friends. You were homecoming *and* prom queen. And *you* got good grades, too."

"Only because you did my math homework."

Desi remembered that. It had made her feel superior. No matter what happened in her life, she could always console herself that at least she wasn't stupid like Gwen. If she'd made Gwen do her own damned homework maybe Gwen would be able to balance her own damned checkbook.

"I'm sorry, Gwen. Really, really, really sorry."

"For what?"

"For treating you like you're an idiot. For thinking it. For trying to be strong after Grandma died. Except I wasn't strong. It was just easier if I treated you like you were pathetic so I didn't feel so lousy. I'm sorry for being a bully and making fun of you about all the supernatural stuff. I'm sorry about getting in your face about your inheritance. If you wanted to burn every dollar in the middle of Acacia Park, that was your business, not mine. I'm sorry for thinking that if you weren't just like me that made you wrong."

"When you say it like that... Boy, you really are mean." Gwen grabbed Desi's hands. "I'm kidding! You're the best sister in the whole world. I love you so much."

"Do you forgive me? I promise I'll never get in your business again unless you ask."

"Only if you forgive me for letting you get in my business so I don't have to deal with boring stuff. I'm sorry for doing things I know drive you crazy." Tears spilled down her cheeks and she jumped up to grab a box of tissues.

To Desi's dismay she began to cry, too. It was as if all the tears she'd denied herself during her adult life now released. Each time she apologized to Gwen for some small sin, fresh tears fell. When Gwen apologized, she shed more tears. When Gwen said she was hungry and offered to make spinach salads with Grandma's special vinaigrette recipe, Desi cried even harder. Upstairs in the apartment all the family photographs brought more tears. Spike squeaking at her and head-butting her shins made her wail.

How Gwen managed to maneuver in the kitchen

while she blubbered and hiccupped and snuffled, Desi didn't have a clue. All she knew was that by the time the tears finally stopped she felt so light she was amazed her that her feet remained on the floor.

Gwen set a plate of salad in front of Desi. "We've never done that before."

Desi's throat hurt so much she didn't know if she could eat. "What?"

"Cried together. Do you realize I've never seen you cry?" Gwen sat down at the table. "So what are we going to do? How do we get rid of the ghost?"

Desi poked at the salad. It looked and smelled delicious, but she doubted she could swallow. "I need your help. You've met Alec Viho, right? He's going to lead us through a ceremony, a summoning. We have to challenge Skillihorn and force him to go away. It takes four people to make a sacred circle. Buck thinks Grandma needs you to be the fourth person."

"Wow," Gwen breathed, waving a forkful of spinach. Her eyes were so bright with excitement Desi's heart sank. Her sister had no idea how dangerous this was going to be, and Desi wished she could take the invitation back.

Desi and Gwen entered Rampart headquarters, Desi thought it was a fitting end to the oddest day she'd ever spent. Gwen had jumped on the idea of cleansing and purifying. Gwen had closed the store, and they'd ended up at a spa. They'd had steam baths, massages, manis and pedis, facials and seaweed wraps. "We're kicking that ghost's ass and we'll look great doing it," Gwen had said.

Desi had almost spoiled it by complaining about the cost. Then it was as if Grandma whispered in her ear. "Life is for living." Instead of complaining, she'd whipped out her credit card and paid the bill without a peep.

Whether or not they got rid of Skillihorn, Gwen was right. They looked great.

Desi touched the rhinestone butterfly pinned to her sweater. It had been one of Grandma's favorites. It made her feel stronger.

Hearing them enter, Dallas poked his head out of the tech room and, seeing Gwen his eyes lit up. He jumped up and helped her off with her coat.

Ringo too, looked out, from the kitchen doorway. His dark eyes lit on Desi and sparkled with wicked glee. "Wait until you get a whiff of what Alec says you have to drink."

He disappeared before Desi could give him a dirty look. "Where is everybody?" she asked Dallas.

"Pip is on the way, Alec is running a little late, and I haven't heard from Buck. How are you, kid? This will work. Alec knows what he's doing." Dallas kept darting glances at Gwen.

"I'm fine. Nervous, but okay."

The main room was ready for the ceremony. All the movie posters and macabre photos had been taken off the walls. The conference table was moved to the rear, and the chairs were piled atop it. The place was sparkling clean and smelled of lemon polish. There were cameras and audio equipment set up in every corner. Desi sniffed, aware of a sickly rotted vegetation smell. She hoped it wasn't the brew Alec meant for her to drink.

Pippin arrived and she and Gwen had a squeal-fest reunion. After Pippin hugged Desi, Desi saw worry in Pippin's eyes. Dallas was excited about the possibility of catching a full-body apparition on video, Ringo was delighted he was going to make Desi choke down a stinking brew and Gwen was ecstatic about being included in a paranormal ceremony. Only Pippin had the good sense to realize this could all go very wrong.

Gwen couldn't contain her curiosity, "Desi says you have a lot of interesting EVPs in the archives, Dallas. I've only heard EVPs on television shows."

Dallas looked with question at Desi. She made a "go ahead" gesture. Dallas invited Gwen into the tech room.

"I wonder why Dallas doesn't ask her out," Pippin said softly to Desi. "He's so hung up on her. Does he stand a chance?"

Before yesterday, Desi would have said no. But now she knew Gwen was far deeper than Desi had ever realized. Dallas reminded her somewhat of Gwen's late fiancé. Like Jesse he was big and blond, smart, confident, and dedicated. Anything he did, he did full out, no holding back.

"Maybe somebody should give Dallas a nudge," Desi said.

"What would you think about it? With Rampart and everything."

"I think Gwen has a better attitude about the paranormal than I do." She laughed self-consciously.

A cell phone rang and Desi went on alert. Dallas answered, then yelled, "That was Buck. He's leaving his place now. He'll be here in a few minutes."

Desi shivered in anticipation of seeing him again.

BUCK PARKED THE JEEP on the street behind a vintage Porsche 911. He saw Desi's Subaru in the duplex driveway. Knowing she waited inside made his pulse race. The Porsche passenger door opened and the driver stepped out. Even in the poor light Buck recognized Alec by the calm, green aura.

Buck picked up a pistol from the passenger seat and exited the Jeep. It was his personal weapon, but he hadn't fired it in years. The .38 revolver, snub-nosed and compact, had plenty of stopping power, but it was fairly useless beyond a range of ten feet or so. After that it was impossible to aim. He still hadn't decided whom to give it to. John Ringo looked as if he might be familiar with firearms, but Dallas had the drive. Dallas, he decided, wouldn't hesitate to do what had to be done.

Was Desi worth dying for?

Buck knew she was.

He slipped the pistol into his coat pocket and waved at Alec.

Under the streetlamps the sports car gleamed like black water. Buck couldn't help an admiring whistle. "That's some sweet ride, man."

"She's my baby," Alec said with a grin.

Buck walked around the little car with the huge engine, taking in the sleek lines and sexy curves, and the glassy finish that looked inches deep. He bet it looked even better in daylight. "What year is it?"

"Sixty-eight. Not everything is original, but most is. Fella gave it to me about ten years ago after I helped his son. I let my boys work on it when they're very, very good."

Buck stepped onto the sidewalk, unable to take his eyes off the Porsche. He reached out to touch it and suddenly every hair on his body raised and prickled. The air turned thick and heavy. Traffic noise dulled. The streetlamp on the corner brightened and turned hot pink. The bulb blew with a shower of sparks.

An invisible suit of armor clamped around Buck, locking his arms in place, crushing his torso. Alec stiffened. Buck tried to shout a warning but his face was paralyzed. Alec's aura darkened and compacted until it looked like an outline drawn around his body with charcoal. It began to draw toward Buck like mist sucked into a fan. Buck tried to move, tried to escape, but the mist touched him and the crushing weight on his body increased.

Alec collapsed.

The Dark Presence lifted Buck's foot and planted it one step closer to the duplex.

DESI AND PIPPIN stood before the kitchen stove and peered into a pot. The dark green brew bubbled with lazy *bloops* and gassy sighs. Desi half expected to see frogs appear. The counter was littered with the remains of chopped greenery, none of which looked like any herbs she'd ever seen in a grocery store.

"You have to drink that?" Pippin asked.

"Maybe puking is part of the ceremony." Desi gave her friend a worried look. "This has to be one of Ringo's jokes. That's disgusting."

From the tech room a door slammed with wall-shaking force, making both women jump.

Dallas howled, "Nooooo!"

Overhead the fluorescent bulbs brightened turning the plastic panels blinding white. Light leaked in streams, as if pulled by invisible hands. The bulbs began to sizzle and the acrid smell of burning plastic overwhelmed the swampy stench from the pot. The lights went out.

Throughout the duplex the walls shook with the force of fists pounding on the tech room door. Dallas, Ringo and Gwen yelled, demanding help in opening the tech-room door. Before Desi could move, the bulbs blew, plunging the apartment into darkness.

THE DARK PRESENCE marched Buck, now a struggling marionette, up the sidewalk and onto the porch. Both sides of the duplex went dark. With every ounce of strength he possessed, Buck pushed backward, flinging himself off the porch. It caught him in midfall and jerked him forward with teeth-cracking force. He flew into the front door, his feet actually leaving the ground. His arm struck the doorjamb and a sickening crack exploded in his ears as pain exploded from his arm. The clamping energy wavered and Buck fell sideways. It caught him before his broken arm struck the concrete and wrenched him upright. He grabbed the storm door and jerked it open.

The inside door opened at the same time.

Jealousy and pain writhed around Buck's body like black ropy snakes. He saw two female figures in the doorway, but they were blurry, as if he were looking through blocks of frosted glass. He wanted to yell at them to close the door, to shut him out, but the Dark Presence hurled him forward.

As if knowing Buck's pain weakened its strength, the Dark Presence dropped its hold on Buck's broken right arm. The crushing weight increased on the rest of his body. As if through ears filled with glue he heard screams and shouts. He dragged his right hand toward his coat pocket. One leg then another stumped forward, lurching him toward Desi. His right hand fished his coat pocket, the grind of jagged bones sending a searing white-hot pain through him. The pain gave him strength against the Dark Presence. He clutched the .38 and dragged it from the pocket. His arm screamed in agony, every nerve on fire, and his fingers grew numb.

The Dark Presence pushed him toward Desi. He saw her terrified eyes reflected in the terrible glow of Skillihorn's face. Buck saw their mistake. There was too much power here for the ghost to steal. Alec, Dallas, Ringo, Gwen, Pippin—the Dark Presence consumed them all , drawing on every trace of their anger and fear the same way it sucked power from electricity and the air.

It consumed him, drained him. He could not feel his legs or his left arm. His lungs burned for air they could not draw.

All he had left was his love for Desi. His wooden forefinger found the trigger. Through sheer force of will, through the force of his love for her, he forced his arm up and pressed the barrel against his throat.

Chapter Fifteen

Desi shoved Pippin toward the open door, then scrambled after her friend. Her eyes had adjusted to the dark apartment, but the blackness was devouring the light, turning Skillihorn impossibly black, impossibly huge. Its face, twisting and shifting like melting wax, glowed with sickly supernatural light. Buck had disappeared within it. The thing lurched and lunged at her.

"Get out!" she screamed. Desi shoved Pippin again and stumbled to her knee. Her feet tangled in the scramble and she twisted to face the black entity. She stared at Buck's right arm, the only part of his body free of the black shroud. Uncomprehending, her shocked brain registered something in his hand drawing ever closer to the thing's head.

A gun. The barrel disappeared into the miasma of Skillihorn's face.

She screamed "No!" and sprang at it. She grabbed Buck's arm with both hands. A red flash blinded her. The report deafened her.

At the errant gunshot the Dark Presence howled and snatched her throat, lifting her off the ground. She kicked and clawed at unyielding flesh and the thing shoved her against the wall. Her head hit first and she moaned as stars blinded her. Then that awful face loomed within inches of her own. She dug her nails into the fingers that once again choked her.

She cried, "Grandma! Help me, Grandma!"

A kaleidoscope of colors swirled through her head. With only one hand to hold her, the thing couldn't get its thumb on her larynx. It pulled her up again and hanged her, clamping off both her carotid arteries with one massive hand, cutting off the blood flow to her brain.

As the curtain of unconsciousness began to drop down she heard, as clearly as a shout, "Forgive."

"I forgive you, Charles," she gasped. "I forgive you!"

She heard and saw it all. A scream as Veronica's husband burst into the room, a scythe clutched in his hand, his entire body racked with pain and jealousy.

"I only loved you! Never another. Never, never," she cried out.

The hand loosened enough for Desi to drag in air. The hovering face lost some of its form.

"You accused me falsely. You never believed I loved you. *You never believed!* But I forgive you." Where the words or the feelings were coming from, Desi didn't know. She just knew. "You know it too, Charles. You know you were wrong. It was your jealousy, your fear, your belief that I could not, would not, love you. You were wrong. You know it! You knew it then and you know it now. I did love you. You were my only love. I forgive you."

Desi's feet touched the floor. The hand dropped away and she slid down the wall, her gaze fixed on the fading glow. She could see Buck now, his face twisted in pain. The blackness shrank, drawing tighter.

"You don't belong here," Desi said. "Veronica is on the other side. She is at peace. She forgives you. She wants you to be at peace, too. You're forgiven, Charles. Now go."

Buck collapsed, hitting the floor with a boneless thud. He moaned then fell silent and still.

DESI CLUTCHED BUCK'S HAND as she trotted beside the gurney to which the paramedics had strapped him. Before they arrived, Alec had tended to Buck, who had kept muttering, "Thank God, the green is back, man." With the deft sureness of a healer, Alec had splinted the arm and propped up Buck's legs to minimize shock. Desi had seen the swelling and the unnatural angle of Buck's forearm. It made her want to throw up. Now Buck was dazed, barely coherent and in terrible pain.

Before the street filled with emergency vehicles, either Dallas or Ringo had made the gun disappear.

Pippin had spoken for the stunned group, telling first the paramedics and then the responding police officers that the circuit box had blown and in the sudden darkness Buck had tripped over a chair and broken his arm. Pippin was also the cool head who had wrapped Desi in her coat and urged her to button it all the way and turn up the collar so no one could see the bruises forming around her neck. Then, to Dallas's dismay, Pippin dumped Ringo's nasty brew on the living room floor. The disgusting smell covered the lingering cordite from the gunshot.

Gwen had mesmerized the police officers, apologizing prettily as she told them she was scared of the dark. So when the lights went out it was her screams the neighbors had reported. The cops swallowed her story of a panic attack as if it were honey. Both looked as if they wanted to take her home and make sure she was really all right.

Desi leaned close to Buck's ear and whispered, "Oh you stupid, stupid man! You almost killed yourself!"

He opened his eyes. "I love you, too, honey," he rasped. He closed his eyes. The paramedics loaded him into the ambulance.

Desi ran back inside to grab her purse and keys, long enough to hear Ringo's lament, "Damn it. We didn't catch even a second of that on video."

She cocked back her arm, let loose and slugged him in the belly.

"Is IT REALLY GONE?" Desi asked yet again, as she adjusted a pillow beneath Buck's arm. He lay in the middle of her bed, in her house, mellow from the painkillers.

"You keep asking that," he said, the words slightly slurred. "It's gone."

He'd spent the night in the hospital after the doctors set his arm, encased it in a huge cast then loaded him up with painkillers. A parade of police officers had passed through the hospital room, making jokes about Buck's clumsiness and how some guys would do anything for a vacation. Buck introduced Desi as his girlfriend. Desi liked that.

He had to go back in a week to make sure he wouldn't need surgery. When he'd helped Desi bring Buck to her house, Alec had assured her that Buck wouldn't need surgery. His arm would heal fine. Now she believed the shaman. She needed to believe Buck that the Dark Presence was really and truly gone.

"It is definitely gone. You have to trust me, honey. I *know*."

She sat very gently beside him. "That knowing of yours is pretty strong, isn't it?"

His eyelids fluttered as he fought to keep his eyes open. "Yes, it is. When I know I know. I'm never wrong."

"You were going to shoot yourself to stop it. You almost died. I don't know if I can forgive you for that."

"You can," he said with a crooked smile. "You

already have." He sighed and gave up the fight, drifting away.

While he slept, she quietly unpacked her clothes and toiletries. She put her closet back in order. She showered and took her dirty clothes to the basement to start some laundry. Her house belonged to her again. It felt like home. She finally let herself believe the Dark Presence was truly and forever gone.

Worry about her grandmother lingered. She hadn't asked Buck or Alec about Grandma. She hadn't told them that Grandma had helped her during the ghostly attack. Grandma had given her the words of forgiveness. Desi worried, plagued with guilt, that the Dark Presence had swallowed Grandma, dragging her along into whatever hell now contained him. She still got the shakes whenever she remembered Buck nearly killing himself in order to save her. It felt just as bad to realize Grandma might have sacrificed her eternal soul.

She cleaned away dust that had accumulated during her absence and put her computer workstation back in order. Buck continued to sleep. His handsome face drew her light kisses. Not wanting to wake him, she scrubbed the bathroom and the kitchen.

An hour later the doorbell rang. Expecting Gwen to arrive with Spike, she hurried to answer. But it was her neighbor, Annaliese, who stood on the porch. She held a plate with the contents covered by a linen napkin. Desi invited her inside. She pressed a finger against her lips. "Shh," she cautioned. "My boyfriend is taking a nap."

Annaliese's eyes lit up. "That is the problem with vacations. They wear you out! You need a vacation to recover." Chuckling, she handed Desi the plate. "Welcome home. I missed you. You will tell me later about the fun you had with your handsome boyfriend. And show me pictures. Lots of pictures."

Desi lifted the napkin and revealed a prettily arranged mound of freshly baked coconut macaroons studded with chocolate chips. Her eyes widened.

"I hope you like macaroons, Desi. It has been so long since I've made them." She tapped the side of her head. "I had this urge. The sun is shining and my little plum tree is getting buds. Macaroons are perfect for a brand-new spring! I mixed in mini-chocolate chips to make them extra special."

All Desi could say was, "Thank you."

After Annaliese left, Desi set the plate on the breakfast counter and stared at the macaroons. She began to laugh. She laughed until she cried. "Oh, Grandma," she choked out. "Buck was right. You always had a great sense of humor."

She wiped her wet cheeks with the back of her hand. "You can go now, Grandma. I'm okay, really. I guess I was mad at you for leaving me. Mad at Mom and Dad. Mad at God. Now Gwen and I are closer than ever. I know you already like Buck. We'll be good together. I'll make sure of it. So you can go. Thank you so much. Goodbye."

She listened and waited for a sign. She picked up a cookie and bit into its soft chewiness.

It tasted just like what Grandma used to make.

BUCK AWAKENED in the early evening. His eyes were bright and alert. He refused pain medication. Desi helped him off the bed, but he insisted on using the bathroom without any help. Through the closed door, she said, "I hope you don't mind, but when Gwen brought Spike home, I sent her to your place. I gave her your key. She brought you some clothes and your razor and stuff."

"That's cool," he said.

When Buck came out Spike nearly tripped him. Buck flinched away from the doorjamb, and with exaggerated care, bent over to pet the cat.

"Now sit," she said.

"I need to move," he said. "I'm stiff all over."

Not as stiff as he was going to be, she thought with a grin. "Then stand there. I'm going to run you a bath." She wrinkled her nose. "You smell like the hospital." She started water running in the tub.

From the doorway he said, "If you'll get me a plastic bag to wrap up the cast I can take a shower."

"No shower. You might slip and fall." She held her hand under the water and adjusted the knobs until the temperature was just right. "In fact, you're going to be a good boy and let me take care of you until I'm positive you're one hundred percent okay."

"You're kind of bossy," he said, smiling.

"Get used to it." She rose and admired his chest. He wore a pair of green scrub pants they'd given him at the hospital. His chest was sculpted, his skin taut, and his good arm was hard cut with muscle. So very sexy. From the very broad, square shoulders to the lean lines of his waist he was beautiful. He took her breath away. She crossed the bathroom and tugged the drawstring on the pants.

"What—"

"Shh." She hooked her fingers in the waistband and shoved them off his hips. The cotton fabric puddled around his feet. She went hot all over and her nerves tingled. "You have no idea how long I've wanted to see you naked."

He looked down at himself. "Worth the wait?"

"Definitely."

"Going to join me in the bath?"

She made a face at the bulky cast. His poor fingers looked pathetically bruised and swollen peeking out from the plaster. "Can't risk getting the cast wet. But don't worry, you're in for the best bath of your life."

He cupped her chin with his good hand and lifted her face to meet his eyes. "I love you, Desi. More than you will ever know."

Her throat choked up. "I'm hard-headed, but I can learn. I have an eternity to figure it out. Right?" She stood on tiptoes and kissed him lightly on the mouth. "I love you. I'll always love you. In this life and into the next."

* * * * *

*Celebrate 60 years of pure
reading pleasure with Harlequin®!*

*Harlequin Presents® is proud to introduce
its gripping new miniseries,*
THE ROYAL HOUSE OF KAREDES.
*An exquisite coronation diamond, split as a
symbol of a warring royal family's feud, is
missing! But whoever reunites the diamond
halves will rule all....*

*Welcome to eight brand-new titles that unfold to
reveal the stories of kings and queens, princes
and princesses torn apart by pride and power, but
finally reunited by love.*

Step into the world of Karedes with
BILLIONAIRE PRINCE, PREGNANT MISTRESS
*Available July 2009
from Harlequin Presents®.*

ALEXANDROS KAREDES, SNOW DUSTING the shoulders of his leather jacket and glittering like jewels in his dark hair, stood at the door. Maria felt the blood drain from her head.

"Good evening, Ms. Santos."

His voice was as she remembered it. Deep. Husky. Perfect English, but with the faintest hint of a Greek accent. And cold, as cold as it had been that awful morning she would never forget, when he'd accused her of horrible things, called her terrible names....

"Aren't you going to ask me in?"

She fought for composure. Last time they'd faced each other, they'd been on his turf. Now they were on hers. She was in command here, and that meant everything.

"There's a sign on the door downstairs," she said, her tone every bit as frigid as his. "It says, 'No soliciting or vagrants.'"

His lips drew back in a wolfish grin. "Very amusing."

"What do you want, Prince Alexandros?"

A tight smile eased across his mouth and it killed her that even now, knowing he was a vicious, arrogant man, she couldn't help but notice what a handsome mouth it was. Chiseled. Generous. Beautiful, like the rest of him, which made him living proof that beauty could, indeed, be only skin deep.

"Such formality, Maria. You were hardly so proper the last time we were together."

She knew his choice of words was deliberate. She felt her face heat; she couldn't help that but she damned well didn't have to let him lure her into a verbal sparring match.

"I'll ask you once more, your highness. What do you want?"

"Ask me in and I'll tell you."

"I have no intention of asking you in. Tell me why you're here or don't. It's your choice, just as it will be my choice to shut the door in your face."

He laughed. It infuriated her but she could hardly blame him. He was tall—six two, six three—and though he stood with one shoulder leaning against the door frame, hands tucked casually into the pockets of the jacket, his pose was deceptive. He was strong, with the leanly muscled body of a well-trained athlete.

She remembered his body with painful clarity. The feel of him under her hands. The power of him moving over her. The taste of him on her tongue.

Suddenly, he straightened, his laughter gone. "I

have not come this distance to stand in your doorway," he said coldly, "and I am not going to leave until I am ready to do so. I suggest you stand aside and stop behaving like a petulant child."

A petulant child? Was that what he thought? This man who had spent hours making love to her and had then accused her of—of trading her body for profit?

Except it had not been love, it had been sex. And the sooner she got rid of him, the better.

She let go of the doorknob and stepped aside. "You have five minutes."

He strolled past her, bringing cold air and the scent of the night with him. She swung toward him, arms folded. He reached past her, pushed the door closed, then folded his arms, too. She wanted to open the door again but she'd be damned if she was going to get into a who's-in-charge-here argument with him. She was in charge, and he would surely see a tussle over the ground rules as a sign of weakness.

Instead, she looked past him at the big clock above her work table.

"Ten seconds gone," she said briskly. "You're wasting time, your highness."

"What I have to say will take longer than five minutes."

"Then you'll just have to learn to economize. More than five minutes, I'll call the police."

Instantly, his hand was wrapped around her wrist. He tugged her toward him, his dark-chocolate eyes almost black with anger.

"You do that and I'll tell every tabloid shark I can contact about how Maria Santos tried to buy a five-hundred-thousand-dollar commission by seducing a prince." He smiled thinly. "They'll lap it up."

* * * * *

What will it take for this billionaire prince
to realize he's falling in love
with his mistress...?
Look for
BILLIONAIRE PRINCE, PREGNANT MISTRESS
by Sandra Marton
Available July 2009
from Harlequin Presents®.

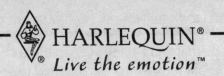

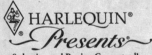

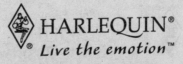

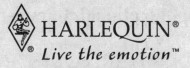

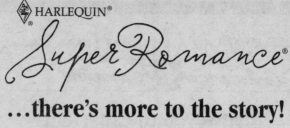
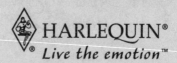

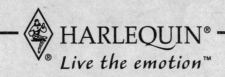

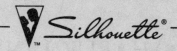

SPECIAL EDITION™

Emotional, compelling stories that capture the intensity of
living, loving and creating a family in today's world.

Desire

Modern, passionate reads that are powerful and provocative.

nocturne

Dramatic and sensual tales of paranormal romance.

Romantic SUSPENSE

Romances that are sparked by danger and fueled by passion.

SDIR07